Penguin Books
The Love Object

Edna O'Brien was born in the West of
Ireland and now lives in London with
her two sons. She has written *The
Country Girls*, *Girl with Green Eyes*,
Girls in their Married Bliss, *August is a
Wicked Month*, and *Casualties of
Peace* (all in Penguins).

Edna O'Brien

The Love Object

Penguin Books

Penguin Books Ltd, Harmondsworth, Middlesex, England
Penguin Books Australia Ltd, Ringwood, Victoria, Australia
Penguin Books Canada Ltd, 41 Steelcase Road West,
Markham, Ontario, Canada

This collection first published by Jonathan Cape 1968
Published in Penguin Books 1970
Reprinted 1972, 1974
Copyright © Edna O'Brien, 1968

'An Outing', 'The Rug', 'Irish Revel', 'Cords' and
'The Love Object' first appeared in the
New Yorker, and the author and publishers are grateful for
permission to include them here.

Made and printed in Great Britain by
Hazell Watson & Viney Ltd
Aylesbury, Bucks
Set in Linotype Baskerville

for Francis Wyndham

As matter desires form
so woman desires man
ARISTOTLE

Contents

The Love Object

He simply said my name. He said 'Martha', and once again I could feel it happening. My legs trembled under the big white cloth and my head became fuzzy, though I was not drunk. It's how I fall in love. He sat opposite. The love object. Elderly. Blue eyes. Khaki hair. The hair was greying on the outside and he had spread the outer grey ribs across the width of his head as if to disguise the khaki, the way some men disguise a patch of baldness. He had what I call a very religious smile. An inner smile that came on and off, governed as it were by his private joy in what he heard or saw: a remark I made, the waiter removing the cold dinner plates that served as ornament and bringing warmed ones of a different design, the nylon curtain blowing inwards and brushing my bare, summer-riped arm. It was the end of a warm, London, summer.

'I'm not mad about them either,' he said. We were engaged in a bit of backbiting. Discussing a famous couple we both knew. He kept his hands joined all the time as if they were being put to prayer. There were no barriers between us. We were strangers. I am a television announcer; we had met to do a job and out of courtesy he asked me to dinner. He told me about his wife – who was thirty like me – and how he knew he would marry her the very first moment he set eyes on her. (She was his third wife.) I made no inquiries as to

9

what she looked like. I still don't know. The only memory I have of her is of her arms sheathed in big, mauve, crocheted sleeves and the image runs away with me and I see his pink, praying hands vanishing into those sleeves and the two of them waltzing in some large, grim room, smiling rapturously at their good fortune in being together. But that came much later.

We had a pleasant supper and figs for afters. The first figs I'd ever tasted. He tested them gently with his fingers, then put three on my side plate. I kept staring down at their purple-black skins, because with the shaking I could not trust myself to peel them. He took my mind off my nervousness by telling me a little story about a girl who was being interviewed on the radio and admitted to owning thirty-seven pairs of shoes and buying a new dress every Saturday which she later endeavoured to sell to friends or family. Somehow I knew that it was a story he had specially selected for me and also that he would not risk telling it to many people. He was in his way a serious man, and famous, though that is hardly of interest when one is telling about a love affair. Or is it? Anyhow, without peeling it I bit into one of the figs.

How do you describe a taste? They were a new food and he was a new man and that night in my bed he was both stranger and lover, which I used to think was the ideal bed partner.

In the morning he was quite formal but unashamed; he even asked for a clothes brush because there was a smudge of powder on his jacket where we had embraced in the taxi coming home. At the time I had no idea whether or not we would sleep together, but on the whole I felt that we would not. I have never owned a clothes brush. I own books and records and various bottles of scent and beautiful clothes, but I never buy cleaning stuffs or aids for prolonging property. I expect it is improvident, but I just throw things away. Anyhow he dabbed the powder smear with his handkerchief and it came off quite easily. The other thing he needed was a piece of sticking plaster because a new shoe had cut his heel. I looked but there was none left in the tin. My children had cleared it out during the long summer holidays. In fact, for a moment, I saw my two sons throughout those summer days, slouched on chairs, reading comics, riding bicycles, wrestling, incurring cuts which they promptly covered with Elastoplast, and afterwards, when the plasters fell, flaunting the brown-rimmed marks, as proof of their valour. I missed them badly and longed to hold them in my arms – another reason why I welcomed his company. 'There's no plaster left,' I said, not without shame. I thought how he would think me neglectful. I wondered if I ought to explain why my sons were at boarding-school when they were still so young. They were eight and ten. But I didn't. I had ceased to want to tell people the tale of how my marriage had ended and my husband unable to care for two young boys, insisted on boarding-school in order to give them, as he put it, a stabilizing influence. I believed it was done in order to deprive me of the pleasure of their company. I couldn't.

We had breakfast out of doors. The start of another warm day. The dull haze that precedes heat hung from the sky and in the garden next door the sprinklers were already on. My neighbours are fanatic gardeners. He ate three pieces of toast and some bacon. I ate also, just to put him at his ease, though normally I skip breakfast. 'I'll stock up with plaster, clothes brush, and cleaning fluids,' I said. My way of saying, 'You'll come again?' He saw through it straight away. Hurrying down the mouthful of toast he put one of his prayer hands over mine and told me solemnly and nicely that he would not have a mean and squalid little affair with me, but that we would meet in a month or so and he hoped we would become friends. I hadn't thought of us as friends but it was an interesting possibility. I remembered the earlier part of our evening's conversation and his referring to his earlier wives and his older grown-up children and I thought how honest and un-nostalgic he was. I was really sick of sorrows and people multiplying them even to themselves. Another thing he did that endeared him was to fold back the green silk bedspread, a thing I never do myself.

When he left I felt quite buoyant and in a way relieved. It had been nice and there were no nasty after-effects. My face was pink from kissing and my hair tossed from our exertions. I looked a little wanton. Feeling tired from such a broken night's sleep I drew the curtains and got back into bed. I had a nightmare. The usual one where I am being put to death by a man. People tell me that a nightmare is healthy and from that experience I believe it. I wakened calmer than I had been for months and passed the remainder of the day happily.

Two mornings later he rang and asked was there a chance of our meeting that night. I said yes because I was not doing anything and it seemed appropriate to have supper and seal our secret decently. But we started recharging.

'We did have a very good time,' he said. I could feel myself making little petrified moves denoting love, shyness; opening my eyes wide to look at him, exuding trust. This time he peeled the figs for both of us. We positioned our legs so that they touched and withdrew them shortly afterwards, confident that our desires were flowing. He brought me home. I noticed when we were in bed that he had put cologne on his shoulder and that he must have set out to dinner with the hope if not the intention of sleeping with me. I liked the taste of his skin better than the foul chemical and I had to tell him so. He just laughed. Never had I been so at ease with a man. For the record I had slept with four other men but there always seemed to be a distance between us, conversation wise. I mused for a moment on their various smells as I inhaled his, which reminded me of some herb. It was not parsley, not thyme, not mint but some non-existent herb compounded of these three smells. On this second occasion our lovemaking was more relaxed.

'What will you do if you make an avaricious woman out of me?' I asked.

'I will pass you on to someone very dear and suitable,' he said. We coiled together, and with my head on his shoulder I thought of pigeons under the railway bridge near by, who passed their nights nestled together, heads folded into mauve breasts. In his sleep we kissed and murmured. I did not sleep. I never do when I am over-happy, over-unhappy or in bed with a strange man.

Neither of us said, 'Well here we are, having a mean and squalid little affair.' We just started to meet. Regularly. We stopped going to restaurants because of his being famous. He would come to my house for dinner. I'll never forget the flurry of those preparations – putting flowers in vases, changing the sheets, thumping knots out of pillows, trying to cook, putting

The Love Object

on make-up and keeping a hair brush near by in case
he arrived early. The agony of it! It was with difficulty
I answered the doorbell, when it finally rang.

'You don't know what an oasis this is,' he would say.
And then in the hallway he would put his hands on my
shoulders and squeeze them through my thin dress
and say, 'Let me look at you,' and I would hang my
head both because I was overwhelmed and because I
wanted to be. We would kiss, often for a full five minutes. He kissed the inside of my nostrils. Then we
would move to the sitting-room and sit on the chaise-
longue still speechless. He would touch the bone of
my knee and say what beautiful knees I had. He saw
and admired parts of one that no other man had ever
bothered with. Soon after supper we went to bed.

Once he came unexpectedly in the late afternoon
when I was dressed to go out. I was going to the theatre
with another man.

'How I wish I were taking you,' he said.

'We'll go to the theatre one night?' He bowed his
head. We would. It was the first time his eyes looked
sad. We did not make love because I was made up and
had my false eyelashes on and it seemed impractical.
He said, 'Has any man ever told you that to see a
woman you desire when you cannot do a thing about it
leaves you with an ache?'

The ache conveyed itself to me and stayed all
through the theatre. I felt angry for not having gone to
bed with him, and later I regretted it even more, because from that evening onward our meetings were
fewer. His wife, who had been in France with their
children, returned. I knew this when he arrived one
evening in a motor car and in the course of conversation mentioned that his small daughter had that day

14

peed over an important document. I can tell you now
that he was a lawyer.

From then on it was seldom possible to meet at night.
He made afternoon dates and at very short notice. Any
night he did stay he arrived with a travel bag containing toothbrush, clothes brush and a few things a man
might need for an overnight, loveless stay in a provin-
cial hotel. I expect she packed it. I thought how ridiculous. I felt no pity for her. In fact the mention of her
name – it was Helen – made me angry. He said it very
harmlessly. He said they'd been burgled in the middle
of the night and he'd gone down in his pyjamas while
his wife telephoned the police from the extension
upstairs.

'They only burgle the rich,' I said hurriedly, to
change the conversation. It was reassuring to find that
he wore pyjamas with her, when he didn't with me.
My jealousy of her was extreme, and of course grossly
unfair. Still I would be giving the wrong impression if
I said her existence blighted our relationship at that
point. Because it didn't. He took great care to speak
like a single man, and he allowed time after our love-
making to stay for an hour or so and depart at his
leisure. In fact it is one of those after-love sessions that
I consider the cream of our affair. We were sitting on
the bed, naked, eating smoked-salmon sandwiches. I
had lighted the gas fire because it was well into
autumn and the afternoons got chilly. The fire made a
steady, purring noise. It was the only light in the room.
It was the first time he noticed the shape of my face
because he said that up to then my colouring had
drawn all of his admiration. His face and the
mahogany chest and the pictures also looked better.
Not rosy, because the gas fire did not have that kind of

15

glow, but resplendent with a whitish light. The goat-skin rug underneath the window had a special, luxurious softness. I remarked on it. He happened to say that he had a slight trace of masochism, and that often, unable to sleep at night in a bed, he would go to some other room and lie on the floor with a coat over him and fall fast asleep. A thing he'd done as a boy. The image of the little boy sleeping on the floor moved me to enormous compassion and without a word from him I led him across to the goatskin and laid him down. It was the only time our roles were reversed. He was not my father. I became his mother. Soft and totally fearless. Even my nipples, about which I am squeamish, did not shrink from his rabid demands. I wanted to do everything and anything for him. As often happens with lovers my ardour and inventiveness stimulated his. We stopped at nothing. Afterwards, remarking on our achievement – a thing he always did – he reckoned it was the most intimate of all our intimate moments. I was inclined to agree. As we stood up to get dressed he wiped his armpits with the white blouse I had been wearing and asked which of my lovely dresses I would wear to dinner that night. He chose my black one for me. He said it gave him great pleasure to know that although I was to dine with others my mind would ruminate on what he and I had done. A wife, work, the world, might separate us but in our thoughts we were betrothed.

'I'll think of you,' I said.

'And I, of you.'

We were not even sad at parting.

It was after that I had what I can only describe as a dream within a dream. I was coming out of sleep, forcing myself awake, wiping my saliva on the pillow

slip, when something pulled me, an enormous weight
dragged me down into the bed and I thought: I have
become infirm. I have lost the use of my limbs and
this accounts for my listlessness for several months
when I've wanted to do nothing except drink tea and
stare out of the window. I am a cripple. All over.
Even my mouth won't move. Only my brain is ticking
away. My brain tells me that a woman downstairs doing
the ironing is the only one who could locate me but she
might not come upstairs for days, she might think I'm
in bed with a man, committing a sin. From time to
time I sleep with a man but normally I sleep alone.
She'll leave the ironed clothes on the kitchen table,
and the iron itself upright on the floor so that it won't
set fire to anything. Blouses will be on hangers, their
frilled collars white and fluid like foam. She's the sort
of woman who even irons the toes and heels of nylon
stockings. She'll slip away, until Thursday, her next
day in. I feel something at my back, or, strictly speaking tugging at my bedcovers which I have mounted
right up the length of my back to cover my head. For
shelter. And I know now that it's not infirmity that's
dragging me down but a man. How did he get in
there? He's on the inside, near the wall. I know what
he's going to do to me and the woman downstairs won't
ever come to rescue me, she'd be too ashamed or she
might not think I want to be rescued. I don't know
which of the men it is, whether it's the big tall bruiser
that's at the door every time I open it innocently, expecting it's the laundry boy and find it's Him with an
old black carving knife, its edge glittering because he's
just sharpened it on a step. Before I can scream my
tongue isn't mine any more. Or it might be the Other
One. Tall too, he gets me by my bracelet as I slip

between the banisters of the stairs. I've forgotten that I am not a little girl any more and that I don't slip easily between banisters. If the bracelet snapped in two I would have made my escape, leaving him with one half of a gold bracelet in his hand, but my goddam provident mother had a safety chain put on it because it was nine carat. Anyhow he's in the bed. It will go on for ever, the thing he wants. I daren't turn round to look at him. Then something gentle about the way the sheet is pulled down suggests that he might be the New One. The man I met a few weeks ago. Not my type at all, tiny broken veins on his cheeks, and red, actually red hair. We were on a goatskin. But it was raised off the ground, high as a bed. I had been doing most of the loving; breasts, hands, mouth, all yearned to minister to him. I felt so sure, never have I felt so sure of the rightness of what I was doing. Then he started kissing me down there and I came to his lapping tongue and his head was under my buttocks and it was like I was bearing him only there was pleasure instead of pain. He trusted me. We were two people, I mean he wasn't someone on me, smothering me, doing something I couldn't see. I could see. I could have shat on his red hair if I wanted. He trusted me. He stretched the come to the very last. And all the things that I loved up to then, like glass or lies, mirrors and feathers, and pearl buttons, and silk, and willow trees, became secondary compared with what he'd done. He was lying so that I could see it: so delicate, so thin, with a bunch of worried blue veins along its sides. Talking to it was like talking to a little child. The light in the room was a white glow. He'd made me very soft and wet so I put it in. It was quick and hard and forceful and he said, 'I'm not considering you now, I think we've considered

18

you,' and I said that was perfectly true and that I liked him roughing away. I said it. I was no longer a hypocrite, no longer a liar. Before that he had often remonstrated with me, he had said, 'There are words we are not going to use to each other, words such as "Sorry" and "Are You Angry?"' I had used these words a lot. So I think from the gentle shuffle of the bed-covers ⊢ like a request really – that it might be him and if it is I want to sink down and down into the warm, dark, sleepy pit of the bed and stay in it for ever, coming with him. But I am afraid to look in case it is not Him but One of the Others.

When I finally got awake I was in a panic and I had a dreadful urge to telephone him, but though he never actually forbade it, I knew he would have been most displeased.

When something has been perfect, as our last encounter in the gaslight had been, there is a tendency to try hard to repeat it. Unfortunately the next occasion was clouded. He came in the afternoon and brought a suitcase containing all the paraphernalia for a dress dinner which he was attending that night. When he arrived he asked if he could hang up his tails as otherwise they would be very creased. He hooked the hanger on the outer rim of the wardrobe and I remember being impressed by the row of war medals along the top pocket. Our time in bed was pleasant but hasty. He worried about getting dressed. I just sat and watched him. I wanted to ask about his medals and how he had merited them, and if he remembered the war, and if he'd missed his then wife, and if he'd killed people, and if he still dreamt about it. But I asked nothing. I sat there as if I were paralysed.

'No braces,' he said as he held the wide black trousers

19

around his middle. His other trousers must have been supported by a belt.

'I'll go to Woolworths for some,' I said. But that was impractical because he was already in danger of being late. I got a safety pin and fastened the trousers from the back. It was a difficult operation because the pin was not really sturdy enough.

'You'll bring it back?' I said. I am superstitious about giving people pins. He took some time to reply because he was muttering 'damn' under his breath. Not to me. But to the stiff, inhuman, starched collar which would not yield to the little gold studs he had wanted to pierce through. I tried. He tried. Each time when one of us failed the other became impatient. He said if we went on the collar would be grubby from our hands. And that seemed a worse alternative. I thought he must be dining with very critical people, but of course I did not give my thoughts on the matter. In the end we each managed to get a stud through and he had a small sip of whisky as a celebration. The bow tie was another ordeal. He couldn't do it. I daren't try.

'Haven't you done it before?' I said. I expect his wives – in succession – had done it for him. I felt such a fool. Then a lump of hatred. I thought how ugly and pink his legs were, how repellent the shape of his body which did not have anything in the way of a waist, how deceitful his eyes that congratulated himself in the mirror when he succeeded in making a clumsy bow. As he put on the coat the sound of the medals tinkling enabled me to remark on their music. There was so little I could say. Lastly he donned a white, silk scarf that came below his middle. He looked like someone I did not know. He left hurriedly. I ran with him down the road to help get a taxi, and trying to keep up with him and chatter was not easy. All I can remember is the ghostly sight of the very white scarf swinging back and forth as we rushed. His shoes, which were patent, creaked unsuitably.

'Is it all-male?' I asked.

'No. Mixed,' He replied.

So that was why we hurried. To meet his wife at some appointed place. The hatred began to grow.

He did bring back the safety pin, but my superstition remained because four straight pins with black rounded tops that had come off his new shirt were on my window ledge. He refused to take them. *He* was not superstitious.

Bad moments, like good ones, tend to be grouped together, and when I think of the dress occasion I also think of the other time when we were not in utter harmony. It was on a street; we were searching for a restaurant. We had to leave my house because a friend had come to stay and we would have been obliged to tolerate her company. Going along the street – it was October and very windy – I felt that he was angry with me for having drawn us out into the cold where we could not embrace. My heels were very high and I was ashamed of the hollow sound they made. In a way I felt we were enemies. He looked in the windows of restaurants to see if any acquaintances of his were there. Two restaurants he decided against, for reasons best known to himself. One looked to be very attractive. It had orange bulbs inset in the walls and the light came through small squares of iron grating. We crossed the road to look at places on the opposite side. I saw a group of rowdies coming towards us and for something to say – what with my aggressive heels, the wind, traffic going by, the ugly unromantic street, we had run out of agreeable conversation – I asked if he ever felt apprehensive about encountering noisy groups like that, late at night. He said that in fact a few nights before he had been walking home very late and saw such a group coming towards him, and before he even registered fear he found that he had splayed his bunch of keys between his fingers and had his hand, armed with the sharp points of the keys, ready to pull out of his pocket should they have threatened him. I suppose he did it again while we were walking along. Curiously enough I did not feel he was my protector. I only felt that he and I were two people, that there was in the world trouble, violence, sickness, catastrophe, that he faced it in one way, and that I faced it – or to be exact that I shrank from it – in another. We would always be outside one another. In the course of that melancholy thought the group went by and my conjecture about violence was all for nothing. We found a nice restaurant and drank a lot of wine.

Later our love-making, as usual, was perfect. He stayed all night. I used to feel specially privileged on the nights he stayed, and the only little thing that lessened my joy was spasms of anxiety in case he should have told his wife he was at such and such an hotel and her telephoning there and not finding him. More than once I raced into an imaginary narrative where she came and discovered us and I acted silent and ladylike and he told her very crisply to wait outside until he was ready. I felt no pity for her. Sometimes I wondered if we would ever meet or if in fact we had already met on an escalator at some point. Though that was unlikely because we lived at opposite ends of London.

Then to my great surprise the opportunity came. I

was invited to a Thanksgiving party given by an American magazine. He saw the card on my mantel-shelf and said, 'You're going to that, too?' and I smiled and said maybe. Was he? 'Yes,' he said. He tried to make me reach a decision there and then but I was too canny. Of course I would go. I was curious to see his wife. I would meet him in public. It shocked me to think that we had never met in the company of any other person. It was like being shut off ... a little animal locked away. I thought very distinctly of a ferret that a forester used to keep in a wooden box with a sliding top when I was a child, and once of another ferret being brought to mate with it. The thought made me shiver. I mean I got it confused; I thought of white ferrets with their little pink nostrils in the same breath as I thought of him sliding a door back and slipping into my box from time to time. His skin had a lot of pink in it.

'I haven't decided,' I said, but when the day came I went. I took a lot of trouble with my appearance, had my hair set, and wore a virginal attire. Black and white. The party was held in a large room with panelled walls of brown wood; blown-up magazine covers were along the panels. The bar was at one end, under a balcony. The effect was of shrunken barmen in white lost underneath the cliff of the balcony which seemed in danger of collapsing on them. A more unlikely room for a party I have never seen. There were women going around with trays, but I had to go to the bar because there was champagne on the trays and I have a preference for whisky. A man I knew conducted me there and en route another man placed a kiss on my back. I hoped that he witnessed this, but it was such a large room with hundreds of people around that I had no idea where he was. I noticed a dress I quite admired, a mauve dress with very wide, crocheted sleeves. Looking up the length of the sleeves I saw its owner's eyes directed on me. Perhaps she was admiring my outfit. People with the same tastes often do. I have no idea what her face looked like, but later when I asked a girl friend which was his wife she pointed to this woman with the crocheted sleeves. The second time I saw her in profile. I still don't know what she looked like, nor do those eyes into which I looked speak to my memory with anything special, except, perhaps, slight covetousness.

Finally I searched him out. I had a mutual friend walk across with me and apparently introduce us. He was unwelcoming. He looked strange, the flush on his cheekbones vivid and unnatural. He spoke to the mutual friend and virtually ignored me. Possibly to make amends he asked, at length, if I was enjoying myself.

'It's a chilly room,' I said. I was referring of course to his manner. Had I wanted to describe the room I would have used 'grim', or some such adjective.

'I don't know about you being chilly but I'm certainly not,' he said with aggression. Then a very drunk woman in a sack dress came and took his hand and began to slobber over him. I excused myself and went off. He said most pointedly that he hoped he would see me again, some time.

I caught his eye just as I left the party and I felt both sorry for him and angry with him. He looked stunned as if important news had just been delivered to him. He saw me leave with a group of people and I stared at him without the whimper of a smile. Yes, I was sorry for him. I was also piqued. The very next day when we met and I brought it up he did not even remember that a mutual friend had introduced us.

'Clement Hastings!' he said, repeating the man's name. Which goes to show how nervous he must have been.

It is impossible to insist that bad news delivered in a certain manner and at a certain time will have a less awful effect. But I feel that I got my walking papers from him at the wrong moment. For one thing it was morning. The clock went off and I sat up wondering when he had set it. Being on the outside of the bed he was already attending to the push button.

'I'm sorry, darling,' he said.

'Did you set it?' I said, indignant. There was an element of betrayal here as if he'd wanted to sneak away without saying good-bye.

'I must have,' he said. He put his arm around me and we lay back again. It was dark outside and there was a feeling – though this may be memory feeling – of frost.

'Congratulations, you're getting your prize today,' he whispered. I was being given an award for my announcing. I am a television announcer.

'Thank you,' I said. I was ashamed of it. It reminded me of being back at school and always coming first in everything and being guilty about this, but not disciplined enough to deliberately hold back.

'It's beautiful that you stayed all night,' I said. I was stroking him all over. My hands were never still in bed. Awake or asleep I constantly caressed him. Not to excite him, simply to reassure and comfort him and perhaps to consolidate my ownership. There is something about holding on to things that I find therapeutic. For hours I hold smooth stones in the palm of my hand or I grip the sides of an armchair and feel the better for it. He kissed me. He said he had never known anyone so sweet or so attentive. Encouraged I began to do something very intimate. I heard his sighs of pleasure, the 'oy, oy' of delight when he was both indulging it and telling himself that he mustn't. At first I was unaware of his speaking voice.

'Hey,' he said, jocularly, just like that. 'This can't go on, you know.' I thought he was referring to our activity at that moment because of course it was late and he would have to get up shortly. Then I raised my head from its sunken position between his legs and I looked at him through my hair which had fallen over my face. I saw that he was serious.

'It just occurred to me that possibly you love me,' he said. I nodded and pushed my hair back so that he would read it, my testimony, clear and clean upon my face. He put me lying down so that our heads were side by side and he began:

'I adore you, but I'm not in love with you, with my commitments I don't think I could be in love with anyone, it all started gay and light-hearted ...' Those last few words offended me. It was not how I saw it or how I remembered it: the numerous telegrams he sent me saying, 'I long to see you', or, 'May the sun shine on you', the first few moments each time when we met and were overcome with passion, shyness and the shock of being so disturbed by each other's presence. We had even searched in our dictionaries for words to convey the specialness of our regard for each other. He came up with 'cense' which meant to adore or cover with the perfume of love. It was a most appropriate word and we used it over and over again. Now he was negating all this. He was talking about weaving me into his life, his family life ... becoming a friend. He said it, though, without conviction. I could not think of a single thing to say. I knew that if I spoke I would be pathetic, so I remained silent. When he'd finished I stared straight ahead at the split between the curtains, and looking at the beam of raw light coming through I said, 'I think there's frost outside,' and he said that possibly there was, because winter was upon us. We got up and as usual he took the bulb out of the bedside lamp and plugged in his razor. I went off to get breakfast. That was the only morning I forgot about squeezing orange juice for him and I often wonder if he took it as an insult. He left just before nine.

The sitting-room held the traces of his visit. Or, to be precise, the remains of his cigars. In one of the blue, saucer-shaped ashtrays there were thick turds of dark-grey cigar ash. There were also stubs but it was the ash I kept looking at, thinking that its thickness resembled the thickness of his unlovely legs. And once again I experienced hatred for him. I was about to tip the contents of the ashtray into the fire-grate when something stopped me, and what did I do but get an empty lozenge box and with the aid of a sheet of paper lift the clumps of ash in there and carry the tin upstairs. With the movement the turds lost their shapes, and whereas they had reminded me of his legs they were now an even mass of dark-grey ash, probably like the ashes of the dead. I put the tin in a drawer underneath some clothes.

Later in the day I was given my award – a very big silver medallion with my name on it. At the party afterwards I got drunk. My friends tell me that I did not actually disgrace myself but I have a humiliating recollection of beginning a story and not being able to go ahead with it, not because the contents eluded me but because the words became too difficult to pronounce. A man brought me home and after I'd made him a cup of tea I said good night over-properly, then when he was gone I staggered to my bed. When I drink heavily I sleep badly. Wakening, it was still dark outside and straight away I remembered the previous morning, and the suggestion of frost outside, and his cold warning words. I had to agree. Although our meetings were perfect I had a sense of doom impending, of a chasm opening up between us, of someone telling his wife, of souring love, of destruction. And still we hadn't gone as far as we should have gone. There were peaks of joy and of its opposite that we should have climbed to, but the time was not left to us. He had of course said, 'You still have a great physical hold over me,' and that in its way I found degrading. To have gone on making love when he had discarded me would have been repellent. It had come to an end. The thing I kept thinking of was a violet in a wood and how a time comes for it to drop off and die. The frost may have had something to do with my thinking, or rather with my musing. I got up and put on a dressing-gown. My head hurt from the hangover but I knew that I must write to him while I had some resolution. I know my own failings and I knew that before the day was out I would want to re-see him, sit with him, coax him back with sweetness and my overwhelming helplessness.

I wrote the note and left out the bit about the violet. It is not a thing you can put down on paper without seeming fanciful. I said if he didn't think it prudent to see me, then not to see me. I said it had been a nice interlude and that we must entertain good memories of it. It was a remarkably controlled letter. He wrote back promptly. My decision came as a shock he said. Still he admitted that I was right. In the middle of the letter he said he must penetrate my composure and to do so he must admit that above and beyond everything he loved me and would always do so. That of course was the word I had been snooping around for, for months. It set me off. I wrote a long letter back to him. I lost my head. I over-said everything. I testified to loving him, to sitting on the edge of madness in the intervening days, to my hoping for a miracle.

It is just as well that I did not write out the miracle in detail because possibly it is, or was, rather inhuman. It concerned his family.

He was returning from the funeral of his wife and children, wearing black tails. He also wore the white silk scarf I had seen him with, and there was a black, mourning tulip in his buttonhole. When he came towards me I snatched the black tulip, and replaced it with a white narcissus, and he in turn put the scarf around my neck and drew me towards him by holding its fringed ends. I kept moving my neck back and forth within the embrace of the scarf. Then we danced divinely on a wooden floor that was white and slippery. At times I thought we would fall but he said, 'You don't have to worry, I'm with you.' The dance floor was also a road and we were going somewhere beautiful.

For weeks I waited for a reply to my letter but there was none. More than once I had my hand on the telephone, but something cautionary – a new sensation for me – in the back of my mind bade me to wait. To give him time. To let regret take charge of his heart. To let him come of his own accord. And then I panicked. I thought that perhaps the letter had gone astray or had fallen into other hands. I'd posted it of course to the office in Lincoln's Inn where he worked. I wrote another. This time it was a formal note, and with it I enclosed a postcard with the words YES and NO. I asked if he had received my previous letter to kindly let me know by simply crossing out the word which did not apply on my card, and send it back to me. It came back with the NO crossed out. Nothing else. So he had received my letter. I think I looked at the card for hours. I could not stop shaking and to calm myself I took several drinks. There was something so brutal about the card, but then you could say that I had asked for it by approaching the situation in that way. I took out the box with his ash in it and wept over it, and both wanted to toss it out of the window and preserve it for evermore.

In general I behaved very strangely. I rang someone who knew him and asked for no reason at all what she thought his hobbies might be. She said he played the harmonium which I found unbearable news altogether. Then I entered a black patch and on the third day I lost control.

Well, from not sleeping and taking pep pills and whisky I got very odd. I was shaking all over and breathing very quickly the way one might after witnessing an accident. I stood at my bedroom window which is on the second floor and looked at the concrete underneath. The only flowers left in bloom were the hydrangeas, and they had faded to a soft russet which was much more fetching than the harsh pink they were all summer. In the garden next door there were frost hats over the fuchsias. Looking first at the hydrangeas, then at the fuchsias, I tried to estimate the consequences of my jumping. I wondered if the drop were great enough. Being physically awkward I could only conceive of injuring myself fatally, which would be worse because I would then be confined to my bed and imprisoned with the very thoughts that were driving me to desperation. I opened the window and leaned out, but quickly drew back. I had a better idea. There was a plumber downstairs installing central heating – an enterprise I had embarked upon when my lover began to come regularly and we liked walking around naked eating sandwiches and playing records. I decided to gas myself and to seek the help of the plumber in order to do it efficiently. I am aware – someone must have told me – that there comes a point in the middle of the operation when the doer regrets it and tries to withdraw, but cannot. That seemed like an extra note of tragedy that I had no wish to experience. So, I decided to go downstairs to this man and explain to him that I *wanted* to die, and that I was not telling him simply for him to prevent me, or console me, that I was not looking for pity – there comes a time when pity is of no help – and that I simply wanted his assistance. He could show me what to do, settle me down, and – this is absurd – be around to take care of the telephone and the doorbell for the next few hours. Also to dispose of me with dignity. Above all I wanted that. I even decided what I would wear: a long dress, which in fact was the same colour as the hydrangeas in their russet phase and which I've never worn except for a photograph or on television. Before going downstairs, I wrote a note which simply said: 'I am committing suicide through lack of intelligence, and through not knowing, not learning to know, how to live.'

You will think I am callous not to have taken the existence of my children into account. But, in fact, I did. Long before the affair began I had reached the conclusion that they had been parted from me irrevocably by being sent to boarding-school. If you like, I felt I had let them down years before. I thought – it was an unhysterical admission – that my being alive or my being dead made little difference to the course of their lives. I ought to say that I had not seen them for a month, and it is a shocking fact that although absence does not make love less it cools down our physical need for the ones we love. They were due home for their mid-term holiday that very day, but since it was their father's turn to have them, I knew that I would only see them for a few hours one afternoon. And in my despondent state that seemed worse than not seeing them at all.

Well of course when I went downstairs the plumber took one look at me and said, 'You could do with a cup of tea.' He actually had tea made. So I took it and stood there warming my child-sized hands around the barrel of the brown mug. Suddenly, swiftly, I remembered my lover measuring our hands when we were lying in bed and saying that mine were no bigger than his daughter's. And then I had another and less edifying memory about hands. It was the time we met when he was visibly distressed because he'd caught those same daughter's hands in a motor-car door. The fingers had not been broken but were badly bruised, and he felt awful about it and hoped his daughter would forgive him. Upon being told the story I bolted off into an anecdote about almost losing *my* fingers in the door of a new Jaguar I had bought. It was pointless, although a listener might infer from it that I was a boastful and heartless girl. I would have been sorry for any child whose fingers were caught in a motor-car door, but at that moment I was trying to recall him to the hidden world of him and me. Perhaps it was one of the things that made him like me less. Perhaps it was then he resolved to end the affair. I was about to say this to the plumber, to warn him about so-called love often hardening the heart, but like the violets it is something that can miss awfully, and when it does two people are mortally embarrassed. He'd put sugar in my tea and I found it sickly.

'I want you to help me,' I said.

'Anything,' he said. I ought to know that. We were friends. He would do the pipes tastefully. The pipes would be little works of art and the radiators painted to match the walls.

'You may think I will paint these white, but in fact they will be light ivory,' he said. The whitewash on the kitchen walls had yellowed a bit.

'I want to do myself in,' I said hurriedly.

'Good God,' he said, and then burst out laughing. He always knew I was dramatic. Then he looked at me and obviously my face was a revelation. For one thing I could not control my breathing. He put his arm around me and led me into the sitting-room and we had a drink. I knew he liked drink and thought, It's an ill wind that doesn't blow some good. The maddening thing was that I kept thinking a live person's thoughts. He said I had so much to live for. 'A young girl like you – people wanting your autograph, a lovely new car,' he said.

'It's all ...' I groped for the word. I had meant to say 'meaningless' but 'cruel' was the word that came out.

'And your boys,' he said. 'What about your boys?' He had seen photographs of them, and once I'd read him a letter from one of them. The word 'cruel' seemed to be blazing in my head. It screamed at me from every corner of the room. To avoid his glance, I looked down at the sleeve of my angora jersey and methodically began picking off pieces of fluff and rolling them into a little ball.

There was a moment's pause.

'This is an unlucky road. You're the third,' he said.

'The third what?' I said, industriously piling the black fluff into my palm.

'A woman further up, her husband was a bandleader, used to be out late. One night she went to the dance hall and saw him with another girl; she came home and did it straight away.'

'Gas?' I asked, genuinely curious.

'No, sedation,' he said, and was off on another story about a girl who'd gassed herself and was found by him because he was in the house treating dry rot at the time. 'Naked, except for a jersey,' he said, and speculated on why she should be attired like that. His manner changed considerably as he recalled how he went into the house, smelt gas and searched it out.

I looked at him. His face was grave. He had scaled eyelids. I had never looked at him so closely before. 'Poor Michael,' I said. A feeble apology. I was thinking that if he had abetted my suicide he would then have been committed to the memory of it.

'A lovely young girl,' he said, wistful.

'Poor girl,' I said, mustering up pity.

There seemed to be nothing else to say. He had shamed me out of it. I stood up and made an effort at normality – I took some glasses off a side-table and moved in the direction of the kitchen. If dirty glasses are any proof of drinking, then quite a lot of it had been done by me over the past few days.

'Well,' he said and rose and sighed. He admitted to feeling pleased with himself.

As it happened, there would have been a secondary crisis that day. Although my children were due to return to their father, he rang to say that the older boy had a temperature, and since – though he did not say this – he could not take care of a sick child, he would be obliged to bring them to my house. They arrived in the afternoon. I was waiting inside the door, with my face heavily made up, to disguise my distress. The sick boy had a blanket draped over his tweed coat and one of his father's scarves around his face. When I embraced him he began to cry. The younger boy went around the house to make sure that everything was as he had last seen it. Normally I had presents for them on their return home, but I had neglected it on this occasion, and consequently they were a little downcast.

'Tomorrow,' I said.

'Why are there tears in your eyes?' the sick boy asked as I undressed him.

'Because you are sick,' I said, telling a half-truth.

'Oh, Mamsies,' he said, calling me by a name he had used for years. He put his arms around me and we both began to cry. He was my less favourite child, and I felt he was crying for that as well as for the numerous unguessed afflictions that the circumstances of a broken home would impose upon him. It was strange and unsatisfying to hold him in my arms when over the months I had got used to my lover's size – the width of his shoulders, the exact height of his body which obliged me to stand on tiptoe so that our limbs could correspond perfectly. Holding my son, I was conscious only of how small he was and how tenaciously he clung.

The younger boy and I sat in the bedroom and played a game which entailed reading out questions such as 'A River?' 'A Famous Footballer?', and then spinning a disc until it steadied down at one letter and using that letter as the first initial of the river or the famous footballer or whatever the question called for. I was quite slow at it, and so was the sick boy. His brother won easily although I had asked him to let the invalid win. Children are callous.

We all jumped when the heating came on, because the boiler, from the basement just underneath, gave an almighty churning noise, and made the kind of sudden erupting move I had wanted to make that morning when I stood at the bedroom window and tried to pitch myself out. As a special surprise and to cheer me up the plumber had called in two of his mates and between them they got the job finished. To make us warm and happy as he put it, when he came to the bedroom to tell me. It was an awkward moment. I'd avoided him since our morning's drama. At tea-time I'd even left his tea on a tray out on the landing. Would he tell other people how I had asked him to be my murderer. Would he have recognized it as that? I gave him and his friends a drink, and they stood uncomfortably in the children's bedroom and looked at the little boy's flushed face and said he would soon be better. What else could they say!

For the remainder of the evening the boys and I played the quiz game over and over again, and just before they went to sleep I read them an adventure story. In the morning they both had temperatures. I was busy nursing them for the next couple of weeks. I made beef tea a lot and broke bread into it and coaxed them to swallow those sops of savoury bread. They were constantly asking to be entertained. The only thing I could think of in the way of facts were particles of nature lore I had gleaned from one of my colleagues in the television canteen. Even with embellishing, it took not more than two minutes to tell my children: of a storm of butterflies in Venezuela, of animals called sloths who are so lazy they hang from trees and become covered with moss, and of how the sparrows in England sing differently to the sparrows in Paris.

'More,' they would say. 'More, more.' Then we would have to play that silly game again or embark upon another adventure story.

At these times I did not allow my mind to wander, but in the evenings when their father came I used to withdraw to the sitting-room and have a drink. Well that was disastrous. The leisure enabled me to brood, also I have very weak bulbs in the lamps and the dimness gives the room a quality that induces reminiscence. I would be transported back. I enacted various kinds of reunion with my lover, but my favourite one was an unexpected meeting in one of those tiled, in-human, pedestrian subways and running towards each other and finding ourselves at a stairway which said (one in London actually does say), 'To central island only', and laughing as we leaped up those stairs propelled by miraculous wings. In less indulgent phases, I regretted that we hadn't seen more sunsets, or cigarette advertisements, or something, because in memory our numerous meetings became one long uninterrupted state of love-making without the ordinariness of things in between to fasten those peaks. The days, the nights with him, seemed to have been sandwiched into a long, beautiful but single night instead of being stretched to the seventeen occasions it actually was. Ah, vanished peaks. Once I was so sure that he had come into the room that I tore off a segment of an orange I had just peeled, and handed it to him.

But from the other room I heard the low, assured voice of the children's father delivering information with the self-importance of a man delivering dogmas, and I shuddered at the degree of poison that lay between us when we'd once professed to love. Plagued love. Then, some of the feeling I had for my husband transferred itself to my lover, and I reasoned with myself that the letter in which he had professed to love me was sham, that he had merely written it when he thought he was free of me, but finding himself saddled once again, he withdrew, and let me have the postcard. I was a stranger to myself. Hate was welling up. I wished multitudes of humiliation on him. I even plotted a dinner party that I would attend having made sure that he was invited and of snubbing him throughout. My thoughts teetered between hate and the hope of something final between us so that I would be certain of his feelings towards me. Even as I sat in a bus, an advertisement which caught my eye was immediately related to him. It said, 'DON'T PANIC WE MEND, WE ADAPT, WE REMODEL.' It was an advertisement for pearl-stringing. I would mend and with vengeance.

I cannot say when it first began to happen, because that would be too drastic and anyhow I do not know. But the children were back at school, and we'd got over Christmas, and he and I had not exchanged cards. But I began to think less harshly of him. They were

silly thoughts really. I hoped he was having little
pleasures like eating in restaurants, and clean socks, and
red wine the temperature he liked it, and even – yes,
even ecstacies in bed with his wife. These thoughts
made me smile to myself, inwardly, the new kind of
smile I had discovered. I shuddered at the risk he'd run
by seeing me at all. Of course the earlier injured
thoughts battled with these new ones. It was like carrying a taper along a corridor where the draughts are
fierce and the chances of it staying alight pretty meagre.
I thought of him and my children in the same instant,
their little foibles became his: my children telling me
elaborate lies about their sporting feats, his slight puffing when we climbed steps and his trying to conceal it.
The age difference between us must have saddened him.
It was then I think that I really fell in love with him.
His courtship of me, his telegrams, his eventual departure, even our lovemaking were nothing compared with
this new sensation. It rose like sap within me, it often
made me cry, the fact that he could not benefit from it!
The temptation to ring him had passed away.

His phone call came quite out of the blue. It was one
of those times when I debated about answering it or not
because mostly I let it ring. He asked if we could meet,
if, and he said this so gently, my nerves were steady
enough? I said my nerves were never better. That was a
liberty I had to take. We met in a café for tea. Toast
again. Just like the beginning. He asked how I was.
Remarked on my good complexion. Neither of us mentioned the incident of the postcard. Nor did he say
what impulse had moved him to telephone. It may
not have been impulse at all. He talked about his work
and how busy he'd been, and then relayed a little story
about taking an elderly aunt for a drive and driving so

slowly that she asked him to please hurry up because she would have walked there quicker.

'You've recovered,' he said then, suddenly. I looked at his face. I could see it was on his mind.

'I'm over it,' I said, and dipped my finger into the sugar bowl and let him lick the white crystals off the tip of my finger. Poor man. I could not have told him anything else, he would not have understood. In a way it was like being with someone else. He was not the one who had folded back the bedspread and sucked me dry and left his cigar ash for preserving. He was the representative of that one.

'We'll meet from time to time,' he said.

'Of course.' I must have looked dubious.

'Perhaps you don't want to?'

'Whenever you feel you would like to.' I neither welcomed nor dreaded the thought. It would not make any difference to how I felt. That was the first time it occurred to me that all my life I had feared imprisonment, the nun's cell, the hospital bed, the places where one faced the self without distraction, without the crutches of other people – but sitting there feeding him white sugar I thought, I now have entered a cell, and this man cannot know what it is for me to love him the way I do, and I cannot weigh him down with it, because he is in another cell confronted with other difficulties.

The cell reminded me of a convent and for something to say I mentioned my sister the nun.

'I went to see my sister.'

'How is she?' he asked. He had often inquired about her. He used to take an interest in her and ask what she looked like. I even got the impression that he had considered the thought of sleeping with her.

'She's fine,' I said. 'We were walking down a corridor

and she asked me to look around and make sure that there weren't any other sisters looking and then she hoisted her skirts up and slid down the banisters.'

'Dear girl,' he said. He liked that story. The smallest things gave him such pleasure.

I enjoyed our tea. It was one of the least fruitless afternoons I'd had in months, and coming out he gripped my arm and said how perfect it would be if we could get away for a few days. Perhaps he meant it.

In fact we kept our promise. We do meet from time to time. You could say things are back to normal again. By normal I mean a state whereby I notice the moon, trees, fresh spit upon the pavement; I look at strangers and see in their expressions something of my own predicament; I am part of everyday life, I suppose. There is a lamp in my bedroom that gives out a dry crackle each time an electric train goes by and at night I count those crackles because it is the time he comes back. I mean the real he, not the man who confronts me from time to time across a café table, but the man that dwells somewhere within me. He rises before my eyes – his praying hands, his tongue that liked to suck, his sly eyes, his smile, the veins on his cheeks, the calm voice speaking sense to me. I suppose you wonder why I torment myself like this with details of his presence but I need it, I cannot let go of him now, because if I did, all our happiness and my subsequent pain – I cannot vouch for his – will all have been nothing, and nothing is a dreadful thing to hold on to.

An Outing

Mrs Farley was sitting in a bus when she first saw it.
She spotted the price as the bus swerved round the corner and she wondered if it could be possible. A three-piece suite for nine pounds! Perhaps it was nineteen?
Or ninety? All day she thought about it.

Next morning she walked there on her way to work.
Nine pounds it was. Quite a good three-piece suite
covered in dark-green tapestry. Second-hand of course
but not so shabby that you'd know. After all, it could
be one that she'd had in her house for years, ever since
she married. She'd buy it.

Luckily she had a pound in her bag which served as a
deposit. While the man wrote out a receipt she sat on
the armchairs, then on the couch, moving along the
seat to make sure it was thoroughly sprung. How well
it would fit into her front room. In the evenings, she
and Mr Farley would have an armchair each. In May
when Mr Farley went on the boiler-maker's outing she
and her friend would share the couch. It would be perfect. May ... the sun through the windows shining on
the castor-oil plant, and the couch a darker shade of
green with antimacassars to protect it from sun and
greasy hair. There would be a cushion for behind his
back, and with a bit of luck some things would be in
bloom, disguising the creosote-soaked fence. He would
see what a good gardener she was.

'Certainly, madam,' the shop assistant was saying in answer to her question about delivery. They would deliver anything; she could pay as and when she liked.

'Have a look around at other things,' he said. They sold new as well as second-hand furniture.

'I'd love one of those.' She pointed to a display of cut-glass vases that were on a glass-topped table. Even in winter light the chips of cut-glass revealed the colours of a rainbow. Wisteria would go lovely in a tall vase like that. Weepy wisteria. Her favourite flower. A watery blue, faded, rather like a garment that has had repeated washings.

'When I win the pools,' she said, and went off to work smiling to herself.

It was a shocking day. The snow had been on the ground now for eight whole weeks. When it first fell, and at each new fall, it was downy white, but in between it was the colour of Mr Farley's chamber pot as she picked it up for emptying each morning. No fresh vegetables either. Talk of coal and paraffin oil being rationed. London was never able to cope with crises, no planning.

She was doing two houses that morning. In all, she cleaned six houses a week; two on Mondays, Wednesdays and Fridays. She devoted the other days to her own home and consequently it was a little palace. Even her husband admitted it. He saw a lot of houses because he installed boilers. He knew how dirty the average London house was: soot on the window sashes, wainscotings never wiped, television knobs never dusted.

'Well I got a bargain at last,' she said to Mrs Captain Hagerty, her first employer, that morning. Mrs Captain Hagerty was on the telephone complaining about a blanket which she'd bought and which had shrunk.

'It's my lucky year,' Mrs Farley said, taking off her coat, her outside cardigan and her boots. There was no doubt. Mrs Captain Hagerty thought, but that Mrs Farley was more spry. She was still plump, but her face was different: the lines softer, the look in her eye not so heartlessly blue. Could Mrs Farley have found another man? Mrs Captain Hagerty thought not, but she was wrong. Mrs Farley had indeed found a man in her forty-sixth year. They had known each other slightly for years – he lived near by – had chatted at bus stops on and off, and once he let her take his turn in the butcher's. Just before Christmas she realized that she had not seen him for weeks, and for several more weeks she searched for him. She would think of his face, especially at night, when she was tired – his thin, disappointed face and his eye sockets riddled with crow's feet. He worked in a furniture factory, and probably had to keep his eyes constantly screwed up so as not to get sawdust in them. That was the thing about hard work, it showed on your hands, or face, or some part of you.

She'd given up hope of ever seeing him again when in fact they met in a snowfall one day and she rushed to shake hands with him. He'd got thinner but the crow's feet were less pronounced. He'd been sick. Nearly died he said. Suddenly, before she knew what she was doing, she had a hand out saying, 'Don't die on me,' and then they pulled off gloves and gripped hands like two people who had a desperate need to grip. They went for a walk down a side street.

'I saw something about a snowflake on television,' she said to him. 'It's a perfect crystal.'

'I saw that, too,' he said, and squeezed her hand

45

tighter. The snow brushed her cheeks but softly, like petals, and warm tears filled her eyes. They were both in the same predicament, married to people they didn't care for, working all day, home at night, television, bed, alarm clock set for six. She thought it a coincidence that they should both be bordering on forty-six and be keen gardeners. Before a half hour was spent they were in love, and like all clandestine lovers they were already conscious of the risks. It was her dry eyes, he said, that first drew her to him, that day in the butcher's. She admitted that she'd had plenty of occasion to cry, in her time.

'Even now,' he said. Through the film of tears she saw him smile at her and she told him how happy they were going to be.

'Yes, I've had a lot of good fortune lately,' she said to Mrs Captain Hagerty as she mopped up the pool of water under the radiator, which her boots had caused.

Mrs Captain Hagerty was saying in her splendidly authoritative voice into the telephone:

'Is that the manager? Well, this is Mrs Captain Hagerty, yes, it *is* a blanket, strawberry-coloured, it shrunk shockingly. I can't tell you, I mean it's hardly fit for a single bed now ...' Then she listened for a second or two, smiled at the mouthpiece, and in a changed voice said, 'Oh, but how kind, how terribly kind, and you'll collect it ... thank *you*.'

Mrs Captain Hagerty had had her way. A van was on its way to collect the fated blanket which she had boiled by mistake in the copper. She was even willing to listen to Mrs Farley's troubles for a few seconds, although she couldn't tolerate any sordid stories about the change.

'It's a lovely shop,' Mrs Farley was saying. 'It's on the

93 bus route, right at the corner. I spotted this bargain yesterday, off the bus ...'

Mrs Captain Hagerty decided that they might as well have coffee. If she had to listen to some story it was as well to be comfortable. Mrs Farley could make up the time later.

'Green matches everything,' Mrs Captain Hagerty said as she stirred saccharine into her coffee. One had to say something to these people.

'And lovely vases,' Mrs Farley went on. 'Lovely, cut-glass ones, that shimmer.'

Mrs Farley was getting quite lyrical. She hadn't mentioned her womb for weeks.

'And they had ever such a funny card on the counter in front of the vases,' Mrs Farley said, and then blushed as she recited it, the way a child would recite!

> 'Lovely to look at,
> Delightful to hold,
> But if you break me
> Consider me sold.'

'Quite,' Mrs Captain Hagerty said. Enough was enough. She stood up to make some more telephone calls. Mrs Farley had to drink down the last of her coffee hurriedly.

That night, in her small front room, Mrs Farley looked at her husband's face in the faint, blue glow from the television screen and decided she would ask him when he wakened up. Even in dim light her husband was plain: fat, with round, pug-like cheeks and a paunch. Awake or asleep he tried to disguise the paunch by placing folded hands across it, and as far as she was concerned, merely drew attention to it. Yes, she'd ask him. She'd done everything to please him all

47

evening. He'd had steak and kidney pie, a pint of director's bitter from the pub, and the right television channel going. He only tolerated the channel which carried advertisements, insisting that the other lot were socialists. It seemed foolish because he slept through it anyhow, but he was a stubborn man and had to have his way.

'Dan,' she said when she saw him stir. 'D'you know what I was just thinking about? D'you remember the winter of the big freeze and you found a lump of coal on the road and brought it home and it turned out to be ice that was black with soot?'

'I remember it,' he said. It was the only memory they ever resorted to. The ice had melted in the grate, ruining the chopped sticks which Mrs Farley had put there. In the end they'd gone out to a pub to get warm. It was nineteen forty-seven, the year of her first miscarriage. They often went to pubs then and had beer and salt-beef sandwiches.

'Yes, I was just thinking about it,' she said, 'when I was looking at you there asleep. Funny how you think of things for no reason.'

'I remember it,' he said. 'It was in Hartfield Road, just beyond the railway bridge ... I was coming along, very cold it was ...'

From a distance she heard his voice receding into the story and she lowered the television.

'Dan,' she said when he had finished. 'I did something reckless today. I couldn't help it.'

'What reckless?' He was wide awake now, his tongue dampening the corners of his mouth.

'I put a pound down on a three-piece suite.'

'We have all the furniture we need,' he said. 'Still paying for those damn beds, I am.'

A year before Mrs Farley had implored him to get single, divan beds. She wasn't well she said, and would be happier in a single bed. She needed privacy. It inconvenienced him no end.

'A three-piece suite for only four pounds,' she said. 'It is a most beautiful, olive green.'

'It must be worm-eaten, you wouldn't get anything for four pounds.'

'I beat him down,' she said. 'They were asking nine, but I beat him down. I think it was my eyes that did it.' The sleepy salesman hadn't even noticed her.

'I'm not buying it,' he said. 'You can take that for definite.'

'You remember,' she said, 'that you said you might get me an umbrella for my birthday, well, if you're getting me anything, I'd rather have the money.'

If he gave her three pounds and if she did an hour extra for Mrs Captain Hagerty, and skimped on the food for herself, she might have the eight pounds balance by May the 10th, which was the day Mr Farley was going on the outing to Brighton. She'd invited her friend in. They had nowhere to meet, except on the street, and they couldn't do much there except each take off a glove and walk hand-in-hand down a road, and up again. Once or twice they took a bus ride and had a cup of coffee a few miles away in Chelsea, but it didn't feel natural.

They met on Saturdays and by coincidence Mr Farley's outing was planned for a Saturday too. Her friend had promised to spend the whole afternoon with her, and for once he would defy his wife and say he was going to a football match. If she had the three-piece suite by then they could sit next to each other on the couch.

'I made no promises about birthdays or anything else,' Mr Farley was saying. Sulky old pig.

'Oh, forget it,' she said, turning up the television sound. 'If being married for seventeen years means nothing to you I can't help it. I can only feel that there's something the matter somewhere ...' She clattered off towards the kitchen in her old bedroom slippers, mumbling.

'Just a minute now ...' he called, but she went into the kitchen and worked her temper out by tidying the cutlery drawer.

That night when he asked for his rights, Mrs Farley was gratified to be able to say no.

'You look well,' her friend said, when they met the following Saturday. Each time she looked younger. Her cheeks were seasoned like an apple and her eyes shone. There was no telling, of course, about her figure because in winter clothes she was shapeless like everyone else.

'It's my hair,' she said. She'd given herself a home perm and put a little peroxide in the water. If Mr Farley knew he'd kill her, so she had to sit well out of the light.

'Yes,' she said. 'I've been told I have hair the texture of a baby's.'

He touched the permed ends with his finger, and asked how her week had been.

'I love you more than ever.'

'I love *you* more than ever,' he said.

'How's your wife?' she asked.

His wife was attending a National Health psychiatrist, learning after seventeen years of marriage how to be a married woman.

'Not that it matters now to me,' he said, squeezing

Mrs Farley's fingers. Her hands were coarse from all the washing and scrubbing but she'd bought rubber gloves and was taking more care.

'Is she nice-looking?' Mrs Farley asked.

'Not as nice as you,' he said. 'She's nothing to you.'

His wife had been a nurse and Mrs Farley reckoned that she would look down on her, who did for people. At least they'd never meet.

'She's bitter,' he said. 'You know, bitter ... always getting a rub at you.'

Mrs Farley knew it well. Mr Farley did that too.

'Don't remind me of her,' he said. They had arrived at the brick arch under the railway bridge, and she stood with her back to the wall waiting for him to kiss her. The thick, jagged icicles which hung from one corner of the arch were dripping down the wall and underneath the pool of water was re-freezing. She'd taken off one of her jerseys so as not to be too bulky for him.

'I've decided what we'll have the day you come in,' she said as she kissed his cold nose. The poor man had bad circulation.

'What?' he said.

'Pork chops and apple sauce,' she said. 'And bread-and-butter pudding to follow.'

'That will be lovely.'

'You'll see the garden,' she said. She heard herself describe the garden as it would be, wisteria on the fence, peonies in the heart-shaped bed, lily-of-the-valley in the deep grass under the gooseberry bush. And then as he opened her coat and put his arms around her she heard herself describe her own front room and in it the olive-green, three-piece suite figured prominently.

51

There was nothing he said he liked better than a house-proud woman. His wife wouldn't even transfer tea from the packet into a biscuit tin which they used as a caddy. Mrs Farley said a woman like that didn't deserve a home.

'It's time,' he said, kissing her mouth, then her chin, then her neck which had got crêpe with the years.

They began to walk, her hand in his pocket. Sometimes their hips touched. His body was very thin. His hip-bone stuck out.

'We'll have the time of our lives,' she said. She didn't know quite what would happen the day he visited her, but it would be the deciding one in their lives.

'You'll give me pork chops,' he said.

'Two for you and one for me.'

'And a cuddle?' he said.

'I might,' she said. She felt glowy all over, even her toes were no longer numb.

'Oh.' she put out her hand to make sure. It had begun to snow again. Her perm would be ruined.

'Just a minute,' he said, and ran into a paper shop. He came back with something for her head.

'A new paper,' she said. 'That we haven't even read.'

He held it over her as they walked along, keeping step.

'We're extravagant,' she said. They stopped and kissed, using the paper as a shield to dismiss the world. That's what being in love meant.

Three days before Mr Farley's summer outing Mrs Farley celebrated her forty-seventh birthday. A day like any other, she cleaned two houses and hurried home to put on the dinner. Mr Farley hadn't mentioned the birthday that morning, but then he was unbearable in the mornings. She bought a cake just to make the meal resemble a happy occasion. The antimacassars were made, she had paid five pounds on the three-piece suite and if he gave her money instead of an umbrella she could pay the balance by Saturday. She would have it delivered that day and when he came home from his outing he would be too tired to complain. There was one thing she would have to be careful about: her friend's pipe. Mr Farley had a sensitive nose, as he didn't smoke himself. She'd have to get her friend out of the house by five and prop the door back as well as opening the window.

'Is that you, Dad?' She was upstairs when she heard him come in. The 'Dad' was an affectionate word since one of the three times when Mr Farley was almost a father.

'It's me,' he said. She came down in a flowered summer dress, her face newly-freckled, because she'd done a bit of gardening while the dinner was cooking. Afterwards she undressed upstairs, and had a good look at herself in the mirror. If the neighbours knew they would have the Welfare Officer on her.

'Dinner's ready,' she said to Mr Farley, as she got his slippers from under the stairs. He put them on, then walked across to the laid table and put three pound notes on her side plate.

'What's that for?' she asked.

'Well, I got enough hints,' he said.

'No you didn't,' she said, 'and not even a card with it.' She sulked a bit. If she looked too happy he might take the money back. Happiness was the one thing he could not abide.

'What use is a card?' he said.

'I may be sentimental, but don't forget I'm a woman.'

she said. The three-piece suite was hers and she could hardly contain herself with excitement.

After dinner he went out and got a card which had 'To my dear wife' on the outside.

'I suppose I have a lot of the schoolgirl in me,' she said, putting it on the mantelshelf. She was doing everything to humour him. They discussed what shirt he'd wear on the outing and she said she'd make sandwiches in case he got peckish on the journey. They were having lunch, of course, in Brighton.

'Don't fall for any young girl in a bathing-suit,' she said.

'Is that what you think I'll be doing?' he said.

'Well, who knows? A handsome man, fancy free.'

That pleased him. He offered to share some of his beer. That night she couldn't very well refuse him his rights, but it was her friend's body she imagined that circumferenced her own.

Next day when Mrs Captain Hagerty was shopping, Mrs Farley took the opportunity to telephone the furniture shop. She arranged to call in Saturday to pay the balance on the suite and asked if they could deliver it the same morning. The man – she recognized him as the one who took her money each week – said certainly.

On the Friday night she slept badly. For one thing Mr Farley had to be up early to catch the coach at Victoria Station. Also she was in a tremor over her friend's visit. Would he like the lounge? Would the pork chops be a little greasy? What would she wear? She'd offer him a sherry when he first arrived, to break the ice. She thought of the doorbell ringing, of a kiss in the hallway, then walking ahead into the room where the three-piece suite would instantly catch his eye. And thinking of these things she fell fast asleep.

'No, no, no.' She wakened from a nightmare with tears streaming down her face. She'd been dreaming that she met him at a bus stop and his face was more wretched than ever. He couldn't come, he said. His wife had found out and threatened to kill herself. He had to promise never to see Mrs Farley again. In the dream Mrs Farley said she would go to his wife and beg her to show some mercy. She ran to his house although he called after her not to.

His wife turned out to have the long, coarse face of one of the women Mrs Farley worked for.

'If you let me see your husband every Saturday for an hour, I'll scrub your house from top to bottom,' Mrs Farley said. The coarse-faced woman seated on a chair nodded to this and from nowhere a bucket of water and a scrubbing-brush appeared. Mrs Farley knelt in that small room and began to scrub the linoleum which had some sort of pattern. She scrubbed with all her might, knowing that it was bringing her back to her friend. Just when she scrubbed the last corner, a wall receded and the room grew larger, and the more she scrubbed the greater the room became, until finally she was scrubbing a limitless area with no walls in sight. She turned to protest, but the coarse-faced woman had vanished and all she heard was the echo of her own voice cursing and sobbing and begging to be let out. She knew that her friend was at the bus stop waiting for her to come back, and greater than the pain of losing him was the injustice. He would think she had betrayed him. It was then she cried 'No, no, no' in her dream and wakened to find herself in a sweat. She got up and took an aspirin. At least it was a relief to know it was a dream. Her legs quaked as she stood at the window and looked out at the garden that was grey in the oncoming dawn. Sometimes she turned to glance at Mr Farley in case he should be awake. The sheet rose and fell over his paunch – he had thrown off the blanket. He was snoring slightly. Tomorrow he was going away, far away to the seaside, on an outing with thirty other men. Thirty other wives would have a day alone. And it came to her again, the conviction that he would die in exactly four years when he was sixty-six. A man in the flat downstairs had died at sixty-six, and because he too had been fat, and grumpy, and had a paunch, Mrs Farley believed that a similar fate awaited her husband. She would be fifty, not young, but not too old. The widow downstairs had bloomed in the last few months and begun to wear loud colours and sing when she was tidying her kitchen. Guiltily Mrs Farley got back into bed and prayed for sleep. Without sleep her face would look pinched and tomorrow she would need to look nice. She shook. That dream had really unnerved her.

By morning she had composed herself. She cooked a big breakfast for Mr Farley and stood at the gate while he walked out of sight towards the main road. Then she dashed back into the house, washed up, dusted the lounge, made a shopping list. By nine o'clock she was at the furniture shop. The assistant smiled as she came forward with the money. When she had paid he murmured something about not being sure whether they could deliver on a Saturday.

'But you promised, you promised,' she said. 'You've got to deliver it, where's the manager?'

Being easily intimidated the assistant fled to find the manager. She walked back and forth, hit her clenched fists together and finally to distract herself she went across to look at the cut-glass vases. Her face in the mirror of the display table was purple. Bad temper played havoc with her circulation. She held a vase in her hand and with her thumb felt the sharp, cut edges. Her eyes were fixed on the door through which he'd disappeared – if only he'd hurry. The vase she held in her hand cost nine pounds and shivering she put it down. 'Lovely to look at, delightful to hold, but if you break me, consider me sold.' An accident like that could wreck her plans for weeks, to think that the vase cost the same as the three-piece suite, to think there were people who could buy such a thing and run the risk of breaking it.

'Madam, I'm very sorry but I'm afraid we can't.' A sly, unaccommodating person he was.

'You can't,' she said. 'You can't let me down.'

'It's not me, madam, I'd be only too glad. The manager has got on to them now and they say they simply can't.'

'Where is he?' Mrs Farley asked, and instinctively she went towards his office door. She'd get that suite delivered if she had to carry it on her back.

The manager met her halfway across the shop. He wore thick, blue-tinted spectacles and she could not be sure what his attitude was, but he sounded sorry enough.

'Is it very urgent, madam?'

'It's my whole life,' she said, not knowing why she said such a rash thing, and then heard herself telling him an elaborate lie about how her son was graduating as a doctor that day and how his friends were coming in to tea and she wanted something for them to sit on. As a father himself the manager said he understood how she felt, and he would have to do something. Another customer stared, as if Mrs Farley had admitted to some terrible crime, then, when she caught his eye, he slunk away, embarrassed; maybe he thought he might be drawn into an argument or asked to contribute money.

'We can't disappoint your boy on a day like this, can we?' the manager said. Mrs Farley thought it the saddest thing anyone had ever said to her. If Mr Farley was listening, or her friend, she'd die!

The upshot was that the manager got another van from a removal firm who were willing to deliver the stuff. There was an extra charge of a pound. Mrs Farley protested. The manager said she could either wait until Monday and have it delivered free, in the shop van, or settle for the removers. She gave in of course.

The movers arrived in an enormous pantechnicon, and she was worried that some of the neighbours might mention it to Mr Farley and ask if he was moving house or something. That was why, when they pulled up, she asked them could they move their van down the street a little, as it was blocking a motor-car entrance. They were very nice about it.

The men put the three pieces of furniture where she told them and then, half-heartedly, she offered them a cup of tea. That delayed her another twenty minutes. When they were gone she went into the front room to re-affirm what she already knew. The three-piece suite was not a success; it did nothing for the room. It was dark and drab. Mr Farley would be right in thinking that it was a mistake. Frayed threads, dimmed stains, a leftover from someone else's life. What had she been thinking of the day she chose it? Of him, her friend, the man she was going to see in a couple of hours. She got a clothes brush and began to brush the couch carefully, hoping that when she'd done it it would look plush.

She came on a ludo button that was stuck down in one of the corners and for a minute she thought it was a shilling. After she had done it carefully with the clothes brush she got out the vacuum cleaner and cleaned it thoroughly all over.

Just in case anything went wrong, Mrs Farley and her friend had previously arranged to meet outside the pub. When he saw her come towards him he knew there was something amiss. She held her head down and wore her flat, canvas shoes.

'Hello.' He came forward to greet her.

'He didn't go,' she said. 'He got suspicious at the last minute.'

For the two hours Mrs Farley had debated what she should say to her friend. One thing was sure: she dare not have him in the front room because he would catch her out in her boasting. Always when she described that room she described the three-piece suite. What he would see was a drab piece of furniture in a drab room where brown paint prevailed. Mr Farley did his own decorating and insisted on brown because it did not have to be renewed so often. She could not let him see it. He would say she was no better than his wife and she did not want that.

'Don't worry,' he said. 'Come and have a drink.'

'You're all dressed up,' she said. He wore a dark suit, a white shirt and a lovely striped tie. He looked wealthy. He looked like the sort of man who would have a wallet full of fivers and a home with easy chairs, and a piano.

'I'm sorry,' she was saying to his disappointed face.

'We'll have a nice day anyhow,' he told her. He worried if the pound he had would see them through. He had not banked on spending any money other than the drink in the pub when they met and a small bottle of liqueur as a little gift to her.

'What will you have?' He'd brought her into the lounge bar and sat her on a high upholstered couch that circled the wall.

'Anything,' she said. He got her a sherry.

'Cheers,' he said, and pushed her cheeks upwards with his hand until she appeared to be smiling.

'I dreamt about you last night,' she said.

'A nice dream?' He smiled so gently.

'A lovely dream.' She couldn't disappoint him any more.

Mrs Farley insisted on buying lunch. They ate in the restaurant that adjoined the pub and they talked in whispers. It was a lovely place with embossed wall-paper and candlesticks on the tables. Everywhere she looked she saw wall couches and easy, comfortable chairs. He wondered if they put candles into the candle-sticks at night and she said they probably didn't be-cause there wasn't a trace of candlegrease. Under the table they gripped hands every few minutes and looked into each other's eyes, desperate to say something.

The lunch cost over a pound, the amount she had set aside anyhow to get the pork chops and sherry and things. While she was in the ladies' room, he debated whether he should propose pictures, or a bus ride around London, or a short boat trip up the Thames. With his money, it had to be just one of those.

They settled on the pictures. They were both think-ing that they could snuggle down and have a taste of the comfort they might have had in Mrs Farley's front room.

The picture turned out to be an English comedy about crooks, and though the handful of people in the cinema laughed, neither Mrs Farley nor her friend found it funny at all. It bore no relation to their own lives, it had nothing to do with their predicament. They said, when they came out, that it was a pity they'd stayed inside so long as the day was scorching.

'Do I look a show?' she asked. Her mouth was swollen from kisses.

'You look lovely.'

What to do next?

'Let's have a walk by the river, and then tea,' he said. He knew a cheap café up that way.

'Are you superstitious?' she asked. He said not very. She said she'd broken something that day and was afraid she'd break two other things. A splinter from a kitchen cup was in her finger.

'I'd like that black one,' he said. He'd been admiring boats that were moored to the riverside. He'd rather have a boat than a car, he told her.

They'd sail away under arched bridges, over locks, out to a changeless blue sea.

'Is it true that the blue lagoon isn't blue?' she asked.

'We'll go there and see when I get my boat,' he said.

She would wear trousers and a raincoat on the boat, but when they came ashore at Monte Carlo and places she would have flowered dresses.

'You never asked me what I broke,' she said.

'Oh, tell me.'

'A cup.'

'A cup.'

Possibly he thought it was silly but it worried her.

'I'll tell you,' he said. 'Get a couple of old cracked ones and break them and then you won't have anything to worry about.'

The cups reminded them both of home and duty. He would have to go shortly.

By five thirty they had talked and walked for an hour. But they had said nothing. He apologized for the bad picture, she said she was sorry she couldn't bring him in.

'Still we had a grand time,' she said.

'No, we hadn't,' he said. 'I should have thought of something special.'

'What do other people do?' she asked.

'Oh, they go to the seaside, they go to hotels, they go to places,' he said. She was sorry now that she hadn't risked it and told him. He would have understood; it might have brought them closer together. She looked at him with regret, with love, she looked intently to keep his image more distinctly in her mind. She might not see him dressed-up again for ages.

They kissed and made their arrangements for the following Saturday, at their usual place.

As she walked away she did not turn round to wave, in case he might expect a smile. Anyhow he was occupied himself, with taking off his tie and rolling it up neatly. His wife had not seen him go out with it on.

She walked, deep in thought. She'd lost her chance. Her husband would live for ever. She and her friend were fated to walk up and down streets towards the railway bridge, and in the end they would grow tired of walking, and they would return, each to a make-shift home.

The Rug

I went down on my knees upon the brand-new linoleum, and smelled the strange smell. It was rich and
oily. It first entered and attached itself to something in
my memory when I was nine years old. I've since
learned that it is the smell of linseed oil, but coming on
it unexpectedly can make me both a little disturbed
and sad.

I grew up in the west of Ireland, in a grey cut-stone
farmhouse, which my father inherited from his father.
My father came from lowland, better-off farming
people, my mother from the windswept hungry hills
above a great lake. As children, we played in a small
forest of rhododendrons – thickened and tangled and
broken under scratching cows – around the house and
down the drive. The avenue up from the front gates
had such great pot-holes that cars had to lurch off into
the field and out again.

But though all outside was neglect, overgrown with
ragwort and thistle, strangers were surprised when they
entered the house; my father might fritter his life away
watching the slates slip from the outhouse roofs – but,
within, that safe, square, lowland house of stone was
my mother's pride and joy. It was always spotless. It
was stuffed with things – furniture, china dogs, Toby
mugs, tall jugs, trays, tapestries and whatnots. Each of
the four bedrooms had holy pictures on the walls and

a gold overmantel surmounting each fireplace. In the fireplaces there were paper fans or lids of chocolate boxes. Mantelpieces carried their own close-packed array of wax flowers, holy statues, broken alarm clocks, shells, photographs, soft rounded cushions for sticking pins in.

My father was generous, foolish, and so idle that it could only have been some sort of illness. That year in which I was nine and first experienced the wonderful smell, he sold another of the meadows to pay off some debt, and for the first time in many years my mother got a lump of money.

She went out early one morning and caught the bus to the city, and through a summer morning and afternoon she trudged around looking at linoleums. When she came home in the evening, her feet hurting from high heels, she said she had bought some beautiful light-brown linoleum, with orange squares on it.

The day came when the four rolls were delivered to the front gates, and Hickey, our farm help, got the horse and cart ready to bring it up. We all went; we were that excited. The calves followed the cart, thinking that maybe they were to be fed down by the roadside. At times they galloped away but came back again, each calf nudging the other out of the way. It was a warm, still day, the sounds of cars and neighbours' dogs carried very distinctly and the cow lats on the drive were brown and dry like flake tobacco.

My mother did most of the heaving and shoving to get the rolls on to the cart. She had early accepted that she had been born to do the work.

She may have bribed Hickey with the promise of hens to sell for himself, because that evening he stayed in to help with the floor – he usually went over to the village and drank a pint or two of stout. Mama, of course, always saved newspapers, and she said that the more we laid down under the lino the longer it would wear. On her hands and knees, she looked up once – flushed, delighted, tired – and said, 'Mark my words, we'll see a carpet in here yet.'

There was calculation and argument before cutting the difficult bits around the door frames, the bay window, and the fireplace. Hickey said that without him my mother would have botched the whole thing. In the quick flow of argument and talk, they did not notice that it was past my bedtime. My father sat outside in the kitchen by the stove all evening while we worked. Later, he came in and said what a grand job we were doing. A grand job, he said. He'd had a headache.

The next day must have been Saturday, for I sat in the sitting-room all morning admiring the linoleum, smelling its smell, counting the orange squares. I was supposed to be dusting. Now and then I re-arranged the blinds, as the sun moved. We had to keep the sun from fading the bright colours.

The dogs barked and the postman cycled up. I ran out and met him carrying a huge parcel. Mama was away up in the yard with the hens. When the postman had gone, I went up to tell her.

'A parcel?' she said. She was cleaning the hens' trough before putting their food in it. The hens were moiling around, falling in and out of the buckets, pecking at her hands. 'It's just binding twine for the baling machine,' she said. 'Who'd be sending parcels?' She was never one to lose her head.

I said that the parcel had a Dublin postmark – the postman told me that – and that there was some black woolly thing in it. The paper was torn at the corner, and I'd pushed a finger in, fearfully.

Coming down to the house she wiped her hands with a wad of long grass. 'Perhaps somebody in America has remembered us at last.' One of her few dreams was to be remembered by relatives who had gone to America. The farm buildings were some way from the house; we ran the last bit. But, even in her excitement, her careful nature forced her to unknot every length of string from the parcel and roll it up, for future use. She was the world's most generous woman, but was thrifty about saving twine and paper, and candle stumps, and turkey wings and empty pill boxes.

'My God,' she said reverently, folding back the last piece of paper and revealing a black sheepskin hearthrug. We opened it out. It was a half-moon shape and covered the kitchen table. She could not speak. It was real sheepskin, thick and soft and luxurious. She examined the lining, studied the maker's label in the back, searched through the folds of brown paper for a possible letter, but there was nothing at all to indicate where it had come from.

'Get me my glasses,' she said. We read the address again, and the postmark. The parcel had been sent from Dublin two days before. 'Call your father,' she said. He was in bed with rheumatic pains. Rug or no rug, he demanded a fourth cup of tea before he could get up.

We carried the big black rug into the sitting-room and laid it down upon the new linoleum, before the fireplace.

'Isn't it perfect, a perfect colour scheme?' she said. The room had suddenly become cosy. She stood back and looked at it with surprise, and a touch of suspicion.

Though she was always hoping, she never really expected things to turn out well. At nine years old, I knew enough about my mother's life to say a prayer of thanks that at last she had got something she wanted, and without having to work for it. She had a round, sallow face and a peculiarly uncertain, timid smile. The suspicion soon left her, and the smile came out. That was one of her happiest days; I remember it as I remember her unhappiest day to my knowledge – the day the bailiff came, a year later. I hoped she would sit in the newly-appointed room on Sundays for tea, without her apron, with her brown hair combed out, looking calm and beautiful. Outside, the rhododendrons, though wild and broken, would bloom red and purple and, inside, the new rug would lie upon the richly smelling linoleum. She hugged me suddenly, as if I were the one to thank for it all; the hen mash had dried on her hands and they had the mealy smell I knew so well.

For spells during the next few days, my mother racked her brain, and she racked our brains, for a clue. It had to be someone who knew something of her needs and wants – how else could he have decided upon just the thing she needed? She wrote letters here and there, to distant relations, to friends, to people she had not seen for years.

'Must be one of *your* friends,' she would say to my father.

'Oh, probably, probably. I've known a lot of decent people in my time.'

She was referring – ironically, of course – to the many strangers to whom he had offered tea. He liked nothing better than to stand down at the gates on a fair day or a race day, engaging passers-by in conversation and finally bringing someone up to the house for tea and boiled eggs. He had a genius for making friends.

'I'd say that's it,' my father said, delighted to take credit for the rug.

In the warm evenings we sat around the fireplace – we'd never had a fire in that room throughout the whole of my childhood – and around the rug, listening to the radio. And now and then, Mama or Dada would remember someone else from whom the rug might have come. Before a week had passed, she had written to a dozen people – an acquaintance who had moved up to Dublin with a greyhound pup Dada had given him, which greyhound had turned out a winner; an unfrocked priest who had stayed in our house for a week, gathering strength from Mama to travel on home and meet his family; a magician who had stolen Dada's gold watch and never been seen since; a farmer who once sold us a tubercular cow and would not take it back.

Weeks passed. The rug was taken out on Saturdays and shaken well, the new lino polished. Once, coming home early from school, I looked in the window and saw Mama kneeling on the rug saying a prayer. I'd never seen her pray like that, in the middle of the day, before. My father was going into the next county the following day to look at a horse he thought he might get cheap; she was, of course, praying that he would keep his promise and not touch a drink. If he did, he might be off on a wild progress and would not be seen for a week.

He went the next day; he was to stay overnight with relations. While he was away, I slept with Mama, for company, in the big brass bed. I wakened to see a candle flame, and Mama hurriedly putting on her cardigan. Dada had come home? No, she said, but she had been lying awake thinking, and there was something she had to tell Hickey or she would not get a wink of sleep. It was not yet twelve; he might be awake. I didn't want to be left in the dark, I said, but she was already hurrying along the landing. I nipped out of bed, and followed. The luminous clock said a quarter to twelve. From the first landing, I looked over and saw her turning the knob of Hickey's door.

Why should he open his door to her then? I thought; he never let anyone in at any time, keeping the door locked when he was out on the farm. Once we climbed in through the window and found things in such a muddle – his good suit laid out flat on the floor, a shirt soaking in a bucket of dirty green water, a milk can in which there was curdled buttermilk, a bicycle chain, a broken Sacred Heart and several pairs of worn, distorted, cast-off boots – that she resolved never to set foot in it again.

'What the hell is it?' Hickey said. Then there was a thud. He must have knocked something over while he searched for his flashlamp.

'If it's fine tomorrow, we'll cut the turf,' Mama said.

Hickey asked if she'd wakened him at that hour to tell him something he already knew – they discussed it at tea-time.

'Open the door,' she said. 'I have a bit of news for you, about the rug.'

He opened the door just a fraction. 'Who sent it?' he asked.

'That party from Ballinsloe,' she said.

'That party' was her phrase for her two visitors who

had come to our house years before – a young girl, and an older man who wore brown gauntlet gloves. Almost as soon as they'd arrived, my father went out with them in their motor-car. When they returned to our house an hour later, I gathered from the conversation that they had been to see our local doctor, a friend of Dad's. The girl was the sister of a nun, who was headmistress at the convent where my sisters were. She had been crying. I guessed then, or maybe later, that her tears had to do with her having a baby and that Dada had taken her to the doctor so that she could find out for certain if she were pregnant and make preparations to get married. It would have been impossible for her to go to a doctor in her own neighbourhood, and I had no doubt but that Dada was glad to do a favour for the nun, as he could not always pay the fees for my sisters' education. Mama gave them tea on a tray – not a spread with hand-embroidered cloth and bone-china cups – and shook hands with them coolly when they were leaving. She could not abide sinful people.

'Nice of them to remember,' Hickey said, sucking air between his teeth and making bird noises. 'How did you find out?'

'I just guessed,' Mama told him.

'Oh, Christ!' Hickey said, closing his door with a fearful bang and getting back into bed with such vehemence that I could hear the springs revolt.

Mama carried me up the stairs, because my feet were cold, and said that Hickey had not one ounce of manners.

Next day, when Dad came home sober, she told him the story, and that night she wrote to the nun. In due course, a letter came to us – with holy medals and scapulars enclosed for me – saying that neither the nun nor her married sister had sent a gift. I expect the girl had married the man with the gauntlet gloves.

' 'Twill be one of life's mysteries,' Mama said, as she beat the rug against the pier, closed her eyes to escape the dust and reconciled herself to never knowing.

But a knock came on our back door four weeks later, when we were upstairs changing the sheets on the beds. 'Run down and see who it is,' she said.

It was a namesake of Dada's from the village, a man who always came to borrow something – a donkey, or a mowing machine, or even a spade.

'Is your mother in?' he asked, and I went halfway up the stairs and called her down.

'I've come for the rug,' he said.

'What rug?' Mama asked. It was the nearest she ever got to lying. Her breathe caught short and she blushed a little.

'I hear you have a new rug here. Well, 'tis our rug, because my wife's sister sent it to us months ago and we never got it.'

'What are you talking about?' she said in a very sarcastic voice. He was a cowardly man, and it was said that he was so ineffectual he would call his wife in from the garden to pour him a cup of tea. I suppose my mother hoped that she would frighten him off.

'The rug the postman brought here one morning, and handed it to your youngster there.' He nodded at me.

'Oh, that,' Mama said, a little stunned by the news that the postman had given information about it. Then a ray of hope, or a ray of lunacy, must have struck her, because she asked what colour of rug he was inquiring about.

'A black sheepskin,' he said.

The Rug

There could be no more doubt about it. Her whole being drooped – shoulders, stomach, voice, everything.

'It's here,' she said absently, and she went through the hall into the sitting-room.

'Being namesakes and that, the postman got us mixed up,' he said stupidly to me.

She had winked at me to stay there and see he did not follow her, because she did not want him to know that we had been using it.

It was rolled and had a piece of cord around the middle when she handed it to him. As she watched him go down the avenue she wept, not so much for the loss – though the loss was enormous – as for her own foolishness in thinking that someone had wanted to do her a kindness at last.

'We live and learn,' she said, as she undid her apron strings, out of habit, and then retied them slowly and methodically, making a tighter knot.

The Mouth of the Cave

There were two routes to the village. I chose the rougher one to be beside the mountain rather than the sea. It is a dusty ill-defined stretch of road littered with rocks. The rocks that have fallen from the cliff are a menacing shade of red once they have split open. On the surface the cliff appears to be grey. Here and there on its grey-and-red face there are small clumps of trees. Parched in summer, tormented by winds in winter they nevertheless survive, getting no larger or no smaller.

In one such clump of green, just underneath the cliff, I saw a girl stand up. She began to tie her suspenders slowly. She had bad balance because when drawing her knickers on she lost her footing more than once. She put her skirt on by bringing it over her head and lastly her cardigan which appeared to have several buttons. As I came closer she walked away. A young girl in a maroon cardigan and a black skirt. She was twenty or thereabouts. Suddenly and without anticipating it I turned towards home so as to give the impression that I'd simply been having a stroll. The ridiculousness of this hit me soon after and I turned round again and walked towards the scene of her secret. I was trembling, but these journeys have got to be accomplished.

What a shock to find that nothing lurked there, no man, no animal. The bushes had not risen from the

weight of her body. I reckoned that she must have been
lying for quite a time. Then I saw that she, too, was
returning. Had she forgotten something? Did she want
to ask me a favour? Why was she hurrying? I could not
see her face, her head was down. I turned and this time
I ran towards the private road that led to my rented
house. I thought, Why am I running, why am I trembling, why am I afraid? Because she is a woman and so
am I. Because, because? I did not know.

When I got to the courtyard I asked the servant who
had been fanning herself to unchain the dog. Then I
sat out of doors and waited. The flowering tree looked
particularly dramatic, its petals richly pink, its scent
oppressively sweet. The only tree in flower. My servant
had warned me about those particular flowers; she had
even taken the trouble to get the dictionary to impress
the word upon me – *Venodno*, poison, poison petals.
Nevertheless I had the table moved in order to be
nearer that tree and we steadied it by putting folded
cigarette cartons under two of its legs. I told the servant
to lay a place for two. I also decided what we would eat,
though normally I don't, in order to give the days some
element of surprise. I asked that both wines be put on
table, and also those long, sugar-coated biscuits that
can be dipped in white wine and sucked until the
sweetness is drained from them and re-dipped and re-
sucked, indefinitely.

She would like the house. It had simplicity despite its
grandeur. A white house with green shutters and a fan-
light of stone over each of the three downstairs
entrances. A sundial, a well, a little chapel. The walls
and the ceilings were a milky-blue and this, combined
with the sea and sky, had a strange hallucinatory effect
as if sea and sky moved indoors. There were maps

instead of pictures. Around the light bulbs pink shells that over the years had got a bit chipped, but this only added to the informality of the place.

We would take a long time over supper. Petals would drop from the tree, some might lodge on the stone table, festooning it. The figs, exquisitely chilled, would be served on a wide platter. We would test them with our fingers. We would know which ones when bitten into would prove to be satisfactory. She, being native, might be more expert at it than I. One or other of us might bite too avidly and find that the seeds, wet and messy and runny and beautiful, spurted over our chins. I would wipe my chin with my hand. I would do everything to put her at ease. Get drunk if necessary. At first I would talk but later show hesitation in order to give her a chance.

I changed into an orange robe and put on a long necklace made of a variety of shells. The dog was still loose in order to warn me. At the first bark I would have him brought in and tied up at the back of the house where even his whimpering would be unheard.

I sat on the terrace. The sun was going down. I moved to another chair in order to get the benefit of it. The crickets had commenced their incessant near-mechanical din and the lizards began to appear from behind the maps. Something about their deft, stealth-like movements reminded me of her, but everything reminded me of her just then. There was such silence that the seconds appeared to record their own passing. There were only the crickets and, in the distance, the sound of sheep-bells, more dreamlike than a bleat. In the distance, too, the lighthouse, faithfully signalling. A pair of shorts hanging on a hook began to flutter in the first breeze and how I welcomed it, knowing that it heralded night. She was waiting for dark, the embracing dark, the sinner's dear accomplice.

My servant waited out of view. I could not see her but I was conscious of her the way one sometimes is of a prompter in the wings. It irritated me. I could hear her picking up or laying down a plate and I knew it was being done simply to engage my attention. I had also to battle with the smell of lentil soup. The smell though gratifying seemed nothing more than a bribe to hurry the proceedings and that was impossible. Because, according to my conjecture, once I began to eat the possibility of her coming was ruled out. I had to wait.

The hour that followed had an edgy, predictable and awful pattern – I walked, sat on various seats, lit cigarettes that I quickly discarded, kept adding to my drink. At moments I disremembered the cause of my agitation, but then recalling her in dark clothes and downcast eyes I thrilled again at the pleasure of receiving her. Across the bay the various settlements of lights came on, outlining towns or villages that are invisible in daylight. The perfection of the stars was loathsome.

Finally the dog's food was brought forth and he ate as he always does, at my feet. When the empty plate skated over the smooth cobbles – due to my clumsiness – and the full moon so near, so red, so oddly hospitable, appeared above the pines, I decided to begin, taking the napkin out of its ring and spreading it slowly and ceremoniously on my lap. I confess that in those few seconds my faith was overwhelming and my hope stronger than it had ever been.

The food was destroyed. I drank a lot.

Next day I set out for the village but took the sea

road. I have not gone the cliff way ever since. I have often wanted to, especially after work when I know what my itinerary is going to be: I will collect the letters, have one Pernod in the bar where retired colonels play cards, sit and talk to them about nothing. We have long ago accepted our uselessness for each other. New people hardly ever come.

There was an Australian painter whom I invited to supper having decided that he was moderately attractive. He became offensive after a few drinks and kept telling me how misrepresented his countrymen were. It was sad rather than unpleasant and the servant and I had to link him home.

On Sundays and feast days girls of about twenty go by, arms round each other, bodies lost inside dark commodious garments. Not one of them looks at me although by now I am known. She must know me. Yet she never gives me a sign as to which she is. I expect she is too frightened. In my more optimistic moments I like to think that she waits there expecting me to come and search her out. Yet, I always find myself taking the sea road even though I most desperately desire to go the other way.

How to Grow a Wisteria

When they were first married they saw no one. That was his wish. They spent their days in their wooden house, high up, on a mountain. There was snow for four or five months of each year, and in the early morning when the sun shone they sat on the veranda admiring the expanse of white fields, and the pines that were weighed down with snow. Beyond the fields reigned mountains, great mountains. She did not feel lonely in the morning. But at night she sometimes sighed. Stabbed she would be by some small memory – a voice, a song, once it was by the taste of warm beetroot. These stray memories she had no control over, no idea when they might occur. They came like spirits to disconcert her. Even when making love they were capable of intruding. She sometimes asked herself why she had chosen a man who insisted on exile. The answer was easy: his disposition and his face fitted in with some brainless dream of hers. He was someone she would never really know.

The only outsider that came was the village idiot, who cycled up to do the garden. He grinned his way through hoeing and digging, never knowing how to answer her questions. Little questions about his mother, his father, his rusted lady's bicycle, and how he came to possess it. Once he rooted up a creeper, and she laughed and talked to her husband about it incessantly as if it were something of major importance. They planted another.

The seasons brought variety – first a false spring, a premature thaw, then a real one, then the flowers, small and soft like the pupils of eyes, sheep lambing, and the things that they had sowed appearing above the ground. When the rains came the wood swelled, and then when the rains went the wood had a terrible time shrinking and settling down. The creak in the house was unnerving. She was not with child. They no longer got up in the middle of lunch or breakfast or supper and walked to their vast bed in a quiver of passion. They chopped wood, they lit the stove, they kept busy; there is always something to do in a house.

When summer came he took a sleeping bag out of doors, saying nothing. He chose the forest. At first she cried, then she became reconciled to it, but she was always hungry and always cold.

At length, feeling the bleakness himself, he agreed to move into a city but on the understanding that they would live perfectly privately. He went first to find an apartment because it had to be suitable, it had to look out on a stretch of green and in a city that is a difficult to find.

She missed him. It was the first time in years that they had been parted, and when he came back and walked along the dark lane carrying a torch she ran and embraced him. In their embrace there was tenderness and a reconciliation.

The apartment had a high ceiling, double doors and a radiator concealed behind wooden bars. They missed the stove. He fitted up his machines – his tape recorder, his record player, his infra-red lamp. Since they had only one room she made a point of being out a lot to leave him to his solitude. In her walks she came to know the streets, intimately. She knew where ill-fitting slabs of stone caused a ridge in the pavement, the rust stains on the red paper kiosks, nannies, prams; she never looked at those inside the prams. She knew the dogs that were at war with their owners and those that followed meekly on their leashes. One or two people smiled at her. There was one square of houses she found particularly enchanting. They were four-storey houses set well back from the road with a flight of steps leading to the tiled porchways. In this square she studied curtains, gateways and the paintwork, thinking she could tell the life of the house by these external signs. She loved that hour of evening when things perked up as people hurried home with provisions for their dinner. Their urgency excited her. She often hurried with them and then found she was going in the wrong direction. In the daytime she made bus journeys, going from terminus to terminus simply to overhear. When she came home she told her husband all that she had seen and all that she heard and he sometimes laughed because she heard some amusing things.

At Christmas she plucked up courage to invite people to dinner. They owned a gallery where she had passed many pleasant hours. It entailed manoeuvring beforehand and a war afterwards. They did not meet with his approval. The woman confessed to a weakness for leather suitcases and that he found distasteful. They had three sets of guests throughout a winter and only one of these evenings went well.

Christmas again, the anniversary of their betrothal and she left him. She walked out of the house and down the street. There were stars, a moon and a succession of street lights to show the way. The frost which was severe seemed to fix and make permanent her action as the frost had fastened the hoof marks of animals on their mountain walks long before. Her friends drove to his apartment and handed him her note saying that she had gone. 'Peace, peace at last,' was what he had said.

He went back to the mountain and wrote her a chain of letters. They were all abusive, and she could not read them through without succumbing to tears.

She moved to a larger city and got a job in a gallery. The intention was to meet people. She lived modestly well. Her old life and her new life, they could not be more opposing. Things went from one extreme to another. It was all parties and friendship and telephone calls now. Not a week, not a day, not an hour went by but she saw someone or was telephoned by someone and made plans. She had plans it seemed for the rest of her life. Life stories were dropped in her ear and though she felt flattered she was also unable to sleep at night, for all the incidents that crowded in on her.

There were lovers, too, drunken lovers in drunken beds after parties, and the more expedient ones were those who called just before dinner and seduced her in the kitchen or the hallway or wherever they happened to be. There were some well-conducted affairs and presents and bunches of flowers and eating in restaurants. There were all these exciting things but the proper feelings of enjoyment refused to come. In fact something else happened. She was filling up with secret revulsion. 'I need a rest, a rest from people,' she would say, but it was impossible to escape.

At one of her parties a tap flew off a cider-barrel and though the cider gushed ponderously over the floor no one made any attempt to control it. Someone had made bows out of mauve lavatory paper and was passing them round and everyone was laughing about this. She wished that they would all leave, together, at once, and like a swarm of flies.

Then she made a resolution. She tried being with people and not seeing and not hearing. But they got through. They always found some chink. It was not difficult – an insult, a well-placed line of flattery, some new gossip and she was theirs. Theirs to make promises to, theirs to be obligated to, theirs to hide her distaste from. She thought there are not left in the world two people who really like one another. Two parts of her were in deadly enmity, the her that welcomed them in and the her that shrank away from them. It was all terrible and tiring and meaningless.

One evening in a friend's house she overturned a glass of red wine. It pooled into a wide stain and went through the holes of the crocheted cloth. Under the cloth there was red crêpe paper so that the stain – a savage red – was out of all proportion to the amount of wine spilt. She apologized of course and her hostess was more than forgiving. In fact they all moved to another room to rid themselves of its unsightliness.

Next time she disgraced herself in an hotel. A tumbler – there had been whisky in it – simply shot out of her hand and missed the very polished boot of a gentleman passing by. Her friend (a new man) found it very funny.

In a drawing-room just before lunch she kicked some bottles which were put to warm by a hearth. She tried mopping it up with a handkerchief before anyone could see. She even used the corner of her flimsy dress. Just like a child.

After that it became inevitable. No matter where she

went, no matter who she was, it simply had to happen. It began to control her life, her outings. Her friends laughed indulgently. They made jokes as she entered rooms and yet it was always mortifying and always shocking when it occurred. Lying down at night it assailed her. She saw herself spilling her way across rooms, dance floors, countries, continents. In her sleep she spilt and when she wakened she dreaded the encounters of the day, knowing what must happen.

The decision took months to arrive at, but one day it was easy to execute. As easy as the night she left her husband, knowing it was for ever. She had to give up seeing people. She was quite methodical about it. She had blinds put on the windows, asked for the telephone to be removed. That was a wrench. To make matters worse the workmen left her the extension saying she might like it for her kiddies. Though unconnected she feared it was in danger of ringing because it had developed the habit. People wrote. Some assumed that she was having a wicked affair with somebody so notorious that he had to be hidden. They were maddeningly coy about it. When they came she hid, telling herself that the ringing would die down once they had run out of patience. An order was delivered once a week and left on the doorstep. On the doorstep, too, she left the empties, letters for posting and the list of necessities for the following week. To her friends she wrote, 'Thank you for asking me, I wish I could, but at the moment I dare not come out of doors. Perhaps another time, perhaps next year?' Each letter always the same. She could have had them printed but she didn't. Each one she wrote carefully in heavy black ink. She did not wish to offend. They had been friends once and she might meet them again before she died. She knew that it needed only a toothache, a burst pipe or an excess of high spirits to lure her back into the world. 'Not yet, not yet,' she would say resolutely to herself.

The day passed agreeably. There were things to be done. Dust assembles of its own accord. She kept everything spotless. She had a small massage machine which she used on herself twice a day. Its effect was both bracing and relaxing and she used it all over. She dressed for dinner, and each evening had two martinis. During dinner she put on some records and allowed herself to be animated. Otherwise it was quiet, quiet. The quiet, ordered days lay ahead like a foreseeable stretch of path. She had no wish to go out. She had nothing to say, nothing to hear. She had only one quibble: the timing of her affliction. Had it happened sooner the marriage need not have ended and they might have stayed together, two withdrawn people, in a house, on a mountain.

Irish Revel

Mary hoped that the rotted, front tyre would not burst.
As it was, the tube had a slow puncture, and twice she
had to stop and use the pump, maddening, because the
pump had no connexion and had to be jammed on
over the corner of a handkerchief. For as long as she
could remember she had been pumping bicycles, cart-
ing turf, cleaning out-houses, doing a man's work. Her
father and her two brothers worked for the forestry, so
that she and her mother had to do all the odd jobs –
there were three children to care for, and fowl and pigs
and churning. Theirs was a mountainy farm in Ireland,
and life was hard.

But this cold evening in early November she was free.
She rode along the mountain road, between the bare
thorn hedges, thinking pleasantly about the party.
Although she was seventeen this was her first party.
The invitation had come only that morning from Mrs
Rodgers of the Commercial Hotel. The postman
brought word that Mrs Rodgers wanted her down that
evening, without fail. At first, her mother did not wish
Mary to go, there was too much to be done, gruel to be
made, and one of the twins had earache, and was likely
to cry in the night. Mary slept with the year-old twins,
and sometimes she was afraid that she might lie on
them or smother them, the bed was so small. She begged
to be let go.

'What use would it be?' her mother said. To her mother all outings were unsettling – they gave you a taste of something you couldn't have. But finally she weakened, mainly because Mrs Rodgers, as owner of the Commercial Hotel, was an important woman, and not to be insulted.

'You can go, so long as you're back in time for the milking in the morning; and mind you don't lose your head,' her mother warned. Mary was to stay overnight in the village with Mrs Rodgers. She plaited her hair, and later when she combed it it fell in dark crinkled waves over her shoulders. She was allowed to wear the black lace dress that had come from America years ago and belonged to no one in particular. Her mother had sprinkled her with Holy Water, conveyed her to the top of the lane and warned her never to touch alcohol.

Mary felt happy as she rode along slowly, avoiding the pot-holes that were thinly iced over. The frost had never lifted that day. The ground was hard. If it went on like that, the cattle would have to be brought into the shed and given hay.

The road turned and looped and rose; she turned and looped with it, climbing little hills and descending again towards the next hill. At the descent of the Big Hill she got off the bicycle – the brakes were unreliable – and looked back, out of habit, at her own house. It was the only house back there on the mountain, small, whitewashed, with a few trees around it, and a patch at the back which they called a kitchen-garden. There was a rhubarb bed, and shrubs over which they emptied tea-leaves and a stretch of grass where in the summer they had a chicken run, moving it from one patch to the next, every other day. She looked away. She was now free to think of John Roland. He came to their

district two years before, riding a motor-cycle at a
ferocious speed; raising dust on the milk-cloths spread
on the hedge to dry. He stopped to ask the way. He was
staying with Mrs Rodgers in the Commercial Hotel and
had come up to see the lake, which was noted for its
colours. It changed colour rapidly – it was blue and
green and black, all within an hour. At sunset it was
often a strange burgundy, not like a lake at all, but
like wine.

'Down there,' she said to the stranger, pointing to the
lake below, with the small island in the middle of it. He
had taken a wrong turning.

Hills and tiny cornfields descended steeply towards
the water. The misery of the hills was clear, from all
the boulders. The cornfields were turning, it was mid-
summer; the ditches throbbing with the blood-red of
fuchsia; the milk sour five hours after it had been put
in the tanker. He said how exotic it was. She had no
interest in views herself. She just looked up at the
high sky and saw that a hawk had halted in the air
above them. It was like a pause in her life, the hawk
above them, perfectly still; and just then her mother
came out to see who the stranger was. He took off his
helmet and said 'Hello', very courteously. He introduced himself as John Roland, an English painter,
who lived in Italy.

She did not remember exactly how it happened, but
after a while he walked into their kitchen with them
and sat down to tea.

Two long years since; but she had never given up
hoping – perhaps this evening. The mail-car man said
that someone special in the Commercial Hotel expected
her. She felt such happiness. She spoke to her bicycle,
and it seemed to her that her happiness somehow

glowed in the pearliness of the cold sky, in the frosted fields going blue in the dusk, in the cottage windows she passed. Her father and mother were rich and cheerful; the twin had no earache, the kitchen fire did not smoke. Now and then, she smiled at the thought of how she would appear to him – taller and with breasts now, and a dress that could be worn anywhere. She forgot about the rotted tyre, got up and cycled.

The five street lights were on when she pedalled into the village. There had been a cattle fair that day, and the main street was covered with dung. The townspeople had their windows protected with wooden half-shutters and makeshift arrangements of planks and barrels. Some were out scrubbing their own piece of footpath with bucket and brush. There were cattle wandering around, mooing, the way cattle do when they are in a strange street, and drunken farmers with sticks were trying to identify their own cattle in dark corners.

Beyond the shop window of the Commercial Hotel, Mary heard loud conversation, and men singing. It was opaque glass so that she could not identify any of them, she could just see their heads moving about, inside. It was a shabby hotel, the yellow-washed walls needed a coat of paint as they hadn't been done since the time De Valera came to that village during the election campaign five years before. De Valera went upstairs that time, and sat in the parlour and wrote his name with a penny pen in an autograph book, and sympathized with Mrs Rodgers on the recent death of her husband.

Mary thought of resting her bicycle against the porter barrels under the shop window, and then of climbing the three stone steps that led to the hall door, but suddenly the latch of the shop door clicked and she ran in terror up the alley by the side of the shop, afraid it might be someone who knew her father and would say he saw her going in through the public bar. She wheeled her bicycle into a shed and approached the back door. It was open, but she did not enter without knocking.

Two townsgirls rushed to answer it. One was Doris O'Beirne, the daughter of the harness-maker. She was the only Doris in the whole village, and she was famous for that, as well as for the fact that one of her eyes was blue and the other a dark brown. She learnt shorthand and typing at the local technical school, and later she meant to be a secretary to some famous man or other in the Government, in Dublin.

'God, I thought it was someone important,' she said when she saw Mary standing there, blushing, pretty and with a bottle of cream in her hand. Another girl! Girls were two a penny in that neighbourhood. People said that it had something to do with the lime water that so many girls were born. Girls with pink skins, and matching eyes, and girls like Mary with long, wavy hair and good figures.

'Come in, or stay out,' said Eithne Duggan, the second girl, to Mary. It was supposed to be a joke but neither of them liked her. They hated shy mountainy people.

Mary came in carrying cream which her mother had sent to Mrs Rodgers, as a present. She put it on the dresser and took off her coat. The girls nudged each other when they saw her dress. In the kitchen was a smell of cow dung and fried onions.

'Where's Mrs Rodgers?' Mary asked.

'Serving,' Doris said in a saucy voice, as if any fool ought to know. Two old men sat at the table eating.

'I can't chew, I have no teeth,' said one of the men, to Doris. ''Tis like leather,' he said, holding the plate of burnt steak towards her. He had watery eyes and he blinked childishly. Was it so, Mary wondered, that eyes got paler with age, like bluebells in a jar?

'You're not going to charge me for that,' the old man was saying to Doris. Tea and steak cost five shillings at the Commercial.

''Tis good for you, chewing is,' Eithne Duggan said, teasing him.

'I can't chew with my gums,' he said again, and the two girls began to giggle. The old man looked pleased that he had made them laugh, and he closed his mouth and munched once or twice on a piece of fresh, shop bread. Eithne Duggan laughed so much that she had to put a dish-cloth between her teeth. Mary hung up her coat and went through to the shop.

Mrs Rodgers came from the counter for a moment to speak to her.

'Mary, I'm glad you came, that pair in there are no use at all, always giggling. Now first thing we have to do is to get the parlour upstairs straightened out. Everything has to come out of it except the piano. We're going to have dancing and everything.'

Quickly, Mary realized that she was being given work to do, and she blushed with shock and disappointment.

'Pitch everything into the back bedroom, the whole shootin' lot,' Mrs Rodgers was saying as Mary thought of her good lace dress, and of how her mother wouldn't even let her wear it to Mass on Sundays.

'And we have to stuff a goose too and get it on,' Mrs Rodgers said, and went on to explain that the party was in honour of the local Customs and Excise Officer who was retiring because his wife won some money in the Sweep. Two thousand pounds. His wife lived thirty miles away at the far side of Limerick and he lodged in the Commercial Hotel from Monday to Friday, going home for the weekends.

'There's someone here expecting me,' Mary said, trembling with the pleasure of being about to hear his name pronounced by someone else. She wondered which room was his, and if he was likely to be in at that moment. Already in imagination she had climbed the rickety stairs and knocked on the door, and heard him move around inside.

'Expecting you!' Mrs Rodgers said, and looked puzzled for a minute. 'Oh, that lad from the slate quarry was inquiring about you, he said he saw you at a dance once. He's as odd as two left shoes.'

'What lad?' Mary said, as she felt the joy leaking out of her heart.

'Oh, what's his name?' Mrs Rodgers said, and then to the men with empty glasses who were shouting for her. 'Oh all right, I'm coming.'

Upstairs Doris and Eithne helped Mary move the heavy pieces of furniture. They dragged the sideboard across the landing and one of the castors tore the linoleum. She was expiring, because she had the heaviest end, the other two being at the same side. She felt that it was on purpose: they ate sweets without offering her one, and she caught them making faces at her dress. The dress worried her too in case anything should happen to it. If one of the lace threads caught in a splinter of wood, or on a porter barrel, she would have no business going home in the morning. They carried out a varnished bamboo whatnot, a small table, knickknacks and a chamber-pot with no handle which held some withered hydrangeas. They smelt awful.

'How much is the doggie in the window, the one with the waggledy tail?' Doris O'Beirne sang to a white china dog and swore that there wasn't ten pounds' worth of furniture in the whole shibeen.

'Are you leaving your curlers in, Dot, till it starts?' Eithne Duggan asked her friend.

'Oh def.,' Doris O'Beirne said. She wore an assortment of curlers – white pipe-cleaners, metal clips, and pink, plastic rollers. Eithne had just taken hers out and her hair, dyed blonde, stood out, all frizzed and alarming. She reminded Mary of a moulting hen about to attempt flight. She was, God bless her, an unfortunate girl with a squint, jumbled teeth and almost no lips; like something put together hurriedly. That was the luck of the draw.

'Take these,' Doris O'Beirne said, handing Mary bunches of yellowed bills crammed on skewers.

Do this! Do that! They ordered her around like a maid. She dusted the piano, top and sides, and the yellow and black keys; then the surround, and the wainscoting. The dust, thick on everything, had settled into a hard film because of the damp in that room. A party! She'd have been as well off at home, at least it was clean dirt attending to calves and pigs and the like.

Doris and Eithne amused themselves, hitting notes on the piano at random and wandering from one mirror to the next. There were two mirrors in the parlour and one side of the folding fire-screen was a blotchy mirror too. The other two sides were of water-lilies painted on black cloth, but like everything else in the room it was old.

'What's that?' Doris and Eithne asked each other, as they heard a hullabulloo downstairs. They rushed out to see what it was and Mary followed. Over the banisters they saw that a young bullock had got in the hall door and was slithering over the tiled floor, trying to find his way out again.

'Don't excite her, don't excite her I tell ye,' said the old, toothless man to the young boy who tried to drive the black bullock out. Two more boys were having a bet as to whether or not the bullock would do something on the floor when Mrs Rodgers came out and dropped a glass of porter. The beast backed out the way he'd come, shaking his head from side to side.

Eithne and Doris clasped each other in laughter and then Doris drew back so that none of the boys would see her in her curling pins and call her names. Mary had gone back to the room, downcast. Wearily she pushed the chairs back against the wall and swept the linoleumed floor where they were later to dance.

'She's bawling in there,' Eithne Duggan told her friend Doris. They had locked themselves into the bathroom with a bottle of cider.

'God, she's a right-looking eejit in the dress,' Doris said. 'And the length of it!'

'It's her mother's,' Eithne said. She had admired the dress before that, when Doris was out of the room, and had asked Mary where she bought it.

'What's she crying about?' Doris wondered, aloud.

'She thought some lad would be here. Do you remember that lad stayed here the summer before last and had a motor-cycle?'

'He was a Jew,' Doris said. 'You could tell by his nose. God, she'd shake him in that dress, he'd think she was a scarecrow.' She squeezed a blackhead on her

chin, tightened a curling pin which had come loose
and said, 'Her hair isn't natural either, you can see it's
curled.'

'I hate that kind of black hair, it's like a gipsy's,'
Eithne said, drinking the last of the cider. They hid the
bottle under the scoured bath.

'Have a cachou, take the smell off your breath,' Doris
said as she hawed on the bathroom mirror and
wondered if she would get off with that fellow O'Toole,
from the slate quarry, who was coming to the party.

In the front room Mary polished glasses. Tears ran
down her cheeks so she did not put on the light. She
foresaw how the party would be; they would all stand
around and consume the goose, which was now simmering in the turf range. The men would be drunk,
the girls giggling. Having eaten, they would dance, and
sing, and tell ghost stories, and in the morning she
would have to get up early and be home in time to
milk. She moved towards the dark pane of window
with a glass in her hand and looked out at the dirtied
streets, remembering how once she had danced with
John on the upper road to no music at all, just their
hearts beating, and the sound of happiness.

He came into their house for tea that summer's day
and on her father's suggestion he lodged with them for
four days, helping with the hay and oiling all the
farm machinery for her father. He understood
machinery. He put back doorknobs that had fallen off.
Mary made his bed in the daytime and carried up a
ewer of water from the rain-barrel every evening, so
that he could wash. She washed the check shirt he
wore, and that day, his bare back peeled in the sun.
She put milk on it. It was his last day with them. After
supper he proposed giving each of the grown-up chil-

dren a ride on the motor-bicycle. Her turn came last, she felt that he had planned it that way, but it may have been that her brothers were more persistent about being first. She would never forget that ride. She warmed from head to foot in wonder and joy. He praised her as a good balancer and at odd moments he took one hand off the handlebar and gave her clasped hands a comforting pat. The sun went down, and the gorse flowers blazed yellow. They did not talk for miles; she had his stomach encased in the delicate and frantic grasp of a girl in love and no matter how far they rode they seemed always to be riding into a golden haze. He saw the lake at its most glorious. They got off at the bridge five miles away, and sat on the limestone wall, that was cushioned by moss and lichen. She took a tick out of his neck and touched the spot where the tick had drawn one pin-prick of blood; it was then they danced. A sound of larks and running water. The hay in the fields was lying green and ungathered, and the air was sweet with the smell of it. They danced.

'Sweet Mary,' he said, looking earnestly into her eyes. Her eyes were a greenish-brown. He confessed that he could not love her, because he already loved his wife and children, and anyhow he said, 'You are too young and too innocent.'

Next day, as he was leaving, he asked if he might send her something in the post, and it came eleven days later: a black-and-white drawing of her, very like her, except that the girl in the drawing was uglier.

'A fat lot of good, that is,' said her mother, who had been expecting a gold bracelet or a brooch. 'That wouldn't take you far.'

They hung it on a nail in the kitchen for a while and then one day it fell down and someone (probably her mother) used it to sweep dust on to, ever since it was used for that purpose. Mary had wanted to keep it, to put it away in a trunk, but she was ashamed to. They were hard people, and it was only when someone died that they could give in to sentiment or crying.

'Sweet Mary,' he had said. He never wrote. Two summers passed, devil's pokers flowered for two seasons, and thistle seed blew in the wind, the trees in the forestry were a foot higher. She had a feeling that he would come back, and a gnawing fear that he might not.

'Oh it ain't gonna rain no more, no more, it ain't gonna rain no more; How in the hell can the old folks say it ain't gonna rain no more.'

So sang Brogan, whose party it was, in the upstairs room of the Commercial Hotel. Unbuttoning his brown waistcoat, he sat back and said what a fine spread it was. They had carried the goose up on a platter and it lay in the centre of the mahogany table with potato stuffing spilling out of it. There were sausages also and polished glasses rim downwards, and plates and forks for everyone.

'A fork supper' was how Mrs Rodgers described it. She had read about it in the paper; it was all the rage now in posh houses in Dublin, this fork supper where you stood up for your food and ate with a fork only. Mary had brought knives in case anyone got into difficulties.

''Tis America at home,' Hickey said, putting turf on the smoking fire.

The pub door was bolted downstairs, the shutters across, as the eight guests upstairs watched Mrs Rodgers carve the goose and then tear the loose pieces away with her fingers. Every so often she wiped her fingers on a tea-towel.

'Here you are, Mary, give this to Mr Brogan, as he's the guest of honour.' Mr Brogan got a lot of breast and some crispy skin as well.

'Don't forget the sausages, Mary,' Mrs Rodgers said. Mary had to do everything, pass the food around, serve the stuffing, ask people whether they wanted paper plates or china ones. Mrs Rodgers had bought paper plates, thinking they were sophisticated.

'I could eat a young child,' Hickey said.

Mary was surprised that people in towns were so coarse and outspoken. When he squeezed her finger she did not smile at all. She wished that she were at home – she knew what they were doing at home; the boys at their lessons; her mother baking a cake of wholemeal bread, because there was never enough time during the day to bake; her father rolling cigarettes and talking to himself. John had taught him how to roll cigarettes, and every night since he rolled four and smoked four. He was a good man, her father, but dour. In another hour they'd be saying the Rosary in her house and going up to bed: the rhythm of their lives never changed, the fresh bread was always cool by morning.

'Ten o'clock,' Doris said, listening to the chimes of the landing clock.

The party began late; the men were late getting back from the dogs in Limerick. They killed a pig on the way in their anxiety to get back quickly. The pig had been wandering around the road and the car came round the corner; it got run over instantly.

'Never heard such a roarin' in all me born days,'

Hickey said, reaching for a wing of goose, the choicest bit.

'We should have brought it with us,' O'Toole said. O'Toole worked in the slate quarry and knew nothing about pigs or farming; he was tall and thin and jagged. He had bright green eyes and a face like a greyhound; his hair was so gold that it looked dyed, but in fact it was bleached by the weather. No one had offered him any food.

'A nice way to treat a man,' he said.

'God bless us, Mary, didn't you give Mr O'Toole anything to eat yet?' Mrs Rodgers said as she thumped Mary on the back to hurry her up. Mary brought him a large helping on a paper plate and he thanked her and said that they would dance later. To him she looked far prettier than those good-for-nothing towns-girls – she was tall and thin like himself; she had long black hair that some people might think streelish, but not him, he liked long hair and simple-minded girls; maybe later on he'd get her to go into one of the other rooms where they could do it. She had funny eyes when you looked into them, brown and deep, like a bloody bog-hole.

'Have a wish,' he said to her as he held the wishbone up. She wished that she were going to America on an aeroplane and on second thoughts she wished that she would win a lot of money and could buy her mother and father a house down near the main road.

'Is that your brother the Bishop?' Eithne Duggan, who knew well that it was, asked Mrs Rodgers, concerning the flaccid-faced cleric over the fireplace. Unknown to herself Mary had traced the letter J on the dust of the picture mirror, earlier on, and now they all seemed to be looking at it, knowing how it came to be there.

'That's him, poor Charlie,' Mrs Rodgers said proudly, and was about to elaborate, but Brogan began to sing, unexpectedly.

'Let the man sing, can't you,' O'Toole said, hushing two of the girls who were having a joke about the armchair they shared; the springs were hanging down underneath and the girls said that any minute the whole thing would collapse.

Mary shivered in her lace dress. The air was cold and damp even though Hickey had got up a good fire. There hadn't been a fire in that room since the day De Valera signed the autograph book. Steam issued from everything.

O'Toole asked if any of the ladies would care to sing. There were five ladies in all – Mrs Rodgers, Mary, Doris, Eithne, and Crystal the local hairdresser, who had a new red rinse in her hair and who insisted that the food was a little heavy for her. The goose was greasy and undercooked, she did not like its raw, pink colour. She liked dainty things, little bits of cold chicken breast with sweet pickles. Her real name was Carmel, but when she started up as a hairdresser she changed to Crystal and dyed her brown hair red.

'I bet you can sing,' O'Toole said to Mary.

'Where she comes from they can hardly talk,' Doris said.

Mary felt the blood rushing to her sallow cheeks. She would not tell them, but her father's name had been in the paper once, because he had seen a pine-marten in the forestry plantation; and they ate with a knife and fork at home and had oil cloth on the kitchen table, and kept a tin of coffee in case strangers called.

She would not tell them anything. She just hung her head, making clear that she was not about to sing.

In honour of the Bishop, O'Toole put 'Far away in Australia' on the horn gramophone. Mrs Rodgers had asked for it. The sound issued forth with rasps and scratchings and Brogan said he could do better than that himself.

'Christ, lads, we forgot the soup!' Mrs Rodgers said suddenly, as she threw down the fork and went towards the door. There had been soup scheduled to begin with.

'I'll help you,' Doris O'Beirne said, stirring herself for the first time that night, and they both went down to get the pot of dark giblet soup which had been simmering all that day.

'Now we need two pounds from each of the gents,' said O'Toole, taking the opportunity while Mrs Rodgers was away to mention the delicate matter of money. The men had agreed to pay two pounds each, to cover the cost of the drink; the ladies did not have to pay anything, but were invited so as to lend a pleasant and decorative atmosphere to the party, and, of course, to help.

O'Toole went around with his cap held out, and Brogan said that as it was *his* party he ought to give a fiver.

'I ought to give a fiver, but I suppose ye wouldn't hear of that,' Brogan said, and handed up two pound notes. Hickey paid up, too, and O'Toole himself and Long John Salmon – who was silent up to then. O'Toole gave it to Mrs Rodgers when she returned and told her to clock it up against the damages.

'Sure that's too kind altogether,' she said, as she put

it behind the stuffed owl on the mantelpiece, under the Bishop's watchful eye.

She served the soup in cups and Mary was asked to pass the cups around. The grease floated like drops of molten gold on the surface of each cup.

'See you later, alligator,' Hickey said, as she gave him his; then he asked her for a piece of bread because he wasn't used to soup without bread.

'Tell us, Brogan,' said Hickey to his rich friend, 'what'll you do, now that you're a rich man?'

'Oh go on, tell us,' said Doris O'Beirne.

'Well,' said Brogan, thinking for a minute, 'we're going to make some changes at home.' None of them had ever visited Brogan's home because it was situated in Adare, thirty miles away, at the far side of Limerick. None of them had ever seen his wife either, who it seems lived there and kept bees.

'What sort of changes?' someone said.

'We're going to do up the drawing-room, and we're going to have flower-beds,' Brogan told them.

'And what else?' Crystal asked, thinking of all the lovely clothes she could buy with that money, clothes and jewellery.

'Well,' said Brogan, thinking again, 'we might even go to Lourdes. I'm not sure yet, it all depends '

'I'd give my two eyes to go to Lourdes,' Mrs Rodgers said.

'And you'd get 'em back when you arrived there,' Hickey said, but no one paid any attention to him.

O'Toole poured out four half-tumblers of whiskey and then stood back to examine the glasses to see that each one had the same amount. There was always great anxiety among the men, about being fair with drink. Then O'Toole stood bottles of stout in little groups of six and told each man which group was his. The ladies had gin and orange.

'Orange for me,' Mary said, but O'Toole told her not to be such a goody, and when her back was turned he put gin in her orange.

They drank a toast to Brogan.

'To Lourdes,' Mrs Rodgers said.

'To Brogan,' O'Toole said.

'To myself,' Hickey said.

'Mud in your eye,' said Doris O'Beirne, who was already unsteady from tippling cider.

'Well we're not sure about Lourdes,' Brogan said. 'But we'll get the drawing-room done up anyhow, and the flower-beds put in.'

'We've a drawing-room here,' Mrs Rodgers said, 'and no one ever sets foot in it.'

'Come into the drawing-room, Doris,' said O'Toole to Mary, who was serving the jelly from the big enamel basin. They'd had no china bowl to put it in. It was red jelly with whipped egg-white in it, but something went wrong because it hadn't set properly. She served it in saucers, and thought to herself what a rough-and-ready party it was. There wasn't a proper cloth on the table either, just a plastic one, and no napkins, and that big basin with the jelly in it. Maybe people washed in that basin, downstairs.

'Well someone tell us a bloomin' joke,' said Hickey, who was getting fed up with talk about drawing-rooms and flower-beds.

'I'll tell you a joke,' said Long John Salmon, erupting out of his silence.

'Good,' said Brogan, as he sipped from his whiskey glass and his stout glass alternately. It was the only way to drink enjoyably. That was why, in pubs, he'd be much happier if he could buy his own drink and not rely on anyone else's meanness.

'Is it a funny joke?' Hickey asked of Long John Salmon.

'It's about my brother,' said Long John Salmon, 'my brother Patrick.'

'Oh no, don't tell us that old rambling thing again,' said Hickey and O'Toole, together.

'Oh let him tell it,' said Mrs Rodgers who'd never heard the story anyhow.

Long John Salmon began, 'I had this brother Patrick and he died; the heart wasn't too good.'

'Holy Christ, not this again,' said Brogan, recollecting which story it was.

But Long John Salmon went on, undeterred by the abuse from the three men:

'One day I was standing in the shed, about a month after he was buried, and I saw him coming out of the wall, walking across the yard.'

'Oh what would you do if you saw a thing like that,' Doris said to Eithne.

'Let him tell it,' Mrs Rodgers said. 'Go on, Long John.'

'Well it was walking toward me, and I said to myself, "What do I do now?"; 'twas raining heavy, so I said to my brother Patrick, "Stand in out of the wet or you'll get drenched."'

'And then?' said one of the girls anxiously.

'He vanished,' said Long John Salmon.

'Ah God, let us have a bit of music,' said Hickey, who had heard that story nine or ten times. It had neither a beginning, a middle nor an end. They put a record on, and O'Toole asked Mary to dance. He did a lot of fancy steps and capering; and now and then he let out a mad 'Yippee'. Brogan and Mrs Rodgers were dancing too and Crystal said that she'd dance if anyone asked her.

'Come on, knees up Mother Brown,' O'Toole said to Mary, as he jumped around the room, kicking the legs of chairs as he moved. She felt funny: her head was swaying round and round, and in the pit of her stomach there was a nice, ticklish feeling that made her want to lie back and stretch her legs. A new feeling that frightened her.

'Come into the drawing-room, Doris,' he said, dancing her right out of the room and into the cold passage where he kissed her clumsily.

Inside Crystal O'Meara had begun to cry. That was how drink affected her; either she cried or talked in a foreign accent and said, 'Why am I talking in a foreign accent?'

This time she cried.

'Hickey, there is no joy in life,' she said as she sat at the table with her head laid in her arms and her blouse slipping up out of her skirtband.

'What joy?' said Hickey, who had all the drink he needed, and a pound note which he slipped from behind the owl when no one was looking.

Doris and Eithne sat on either side of Long John Salmon, asking if they could go out next year when the sugar plums were ripe. Long John Salmon lived by himself, way up the country, and he had a big orchard. He was odd and silent in himself; he took a swim every day, winter and summer, in the river, at the back of his house.

'Two old married people,' Brogan said, as he put his arm round Mrs Rodgers and urged her to sit down because he was out of breath from dancing. He said he'd go away with happy memories of them all, and sitting down he drew her on to his lap. She was a heavy woman, with straggly brown hair that had once been a nut colour.

'There is no joy in life,' Crystal sobbed, as the gramophone made crackling noises and Mary ran in from the landing, away from O'Toole.

'I mean business,' O'Toole said, and winked.

O'Toole was the first to get quarrelsome.

'Now ladies, now gentlemen, a little laughing sketch, are we ready?' he asked.

'Fire ahead,' Hickey told him.

'Well, there was these three lads, Paddy th'Irishman, Paddy th'Englishman, and Paddy the Scotsman, and they were badly in need of a . . .'

'Now, no smut,' Mrs Rodgers snapped, before he had uttered a wrong word at all.

'What smut?' said O'Toole, getting offended. 'Smut!' And he asked her to explain an accusation like that.

'Think of the girls,' Mrs Rodgers said.

'Girls,' O'Toole sneered, as he picked up the bottle of cream – which they'd forgotten to use with the jelly – and poured it into the carcass of the ravaged goose.

'Christ's sake, man,' Hickey said, taking the bottle of cream out of O'Toole's hand.

Mrs Rodgers said that it was high time everyone went to bed, as the party seemed to be over.

The guests would spend the night in the Commercial. It was too late for them to go home anyhow, and also Mrs Rodgers did not want them to be observed staggering out of the house at that hour. The police watched her like hawks and she didn't want any trouble, until Christmas was over at least. The sleeping arrangements had been decided earlier on – there were three bedrooms vacant. One was Brogan's, the room he always slept in. The other three men were to pitch in together in the second big bedroom, and the girls were to share the back room with Mrs Rodgers herself.

'Come on, everyone, blanket street,' Mrs Rodgers said, as she put a guard in front of the dying fire and took the money from behind the owl.

'Sugar you,' O'Toole said, pouring stout now into the carcass of the goose, and Long John Salmon wished that he had never come. He thought of daylight and of his swim in the mountain river at the back of his grey, stone house.

'Ablution,' he said, aloud, taking pleasure in the word and in thought of the cold water touching him. He could do without people, people were waste. He remembered catkins on a tree outside his window, catkins in February as white as snow; who needed people?

'Crystal, stir yourself,' Hickey said, as he put on her shoes and patted the calves of her legs.

Brogan kissed the four girls and saw them across the landing to the bedroom. Mary was glad to escape without O'Toole noticing; he was very obstreperous and Hickey was trying to control him.

In the bedroom she sighed; she had forgotten all about the furniture being pitched in there. Wearily they began to unload the things. The room was so crammed that they could hardly move in it. Mary suddenly felt alert and frightened, because O'Toole could be heard yelling and singing out on the landing. There had been gin in her orangeade, she knew now, because she breathed closely on to the palm of her hand and smelt her own breath. She had broken her Confirmation pledge, broken her promise; it would bring her bad luck.

Mrs Rodgers came in and said that five of them would be too crushed in the bed, so that she herself would sleep on the sofa for one night.

'Two of you at the top and two at the bottom,' she said, as she warned them not to break any of the ornaments, and not to stay talking all night.

'Night and God bless,' she said, as she shut the door behind her.

'Nice thing,' said Doris O'Beirne, 'bunging us all in here; I wonder where she's off to?'

'Will you loan me curlers?' Crystal asked. To Crystal, hair was the most important thing on earth. She would never get married because you couldn't wear curlers in bed then. Eithne Duggan said she wouldn't put curlers in now if she got five million for doing it, she was that jaded. She threw herself down on the quilt and spread her arms out. She was a noisy, sweaty girl but Mary liked her better than the other two.

'Ah me old segotums,' O'Toole said, pushing their door in. The girls exclaimed and asked him to go out at once as they were preparing for bed.

'Come into the drawing-room, Doris,' he said to Mary, and curled his forefinger at her. He was drunk and couldn't focus her properly but he knew that she was standing there somewhere.

'Go to bed, you're drunk,' Doris O'Beirne said, and he stood very upright for an instant and asked her to speak for herself.

'Go to bed, Michael, you're tired,' Mary said to him. She tried to sound calm because he looked so wild.

'Come into the drawing-room, I tell you,' he said, as he caught her wrist and dragged her towards the door.

She let out a cry, and Eithne Duggan said she'd brain him if he didn't leave the girl alone.

'Give me that flower-pot, Doris,' Eithne Duggan called, and then Mary began to cry in case there might be a scene. She hated scenes. Once she heard her father and a neighbour having a row about boundary rights and she'd never forgotten it; they had both been a bit drunk, after a fair.

'Are you cracked or are you mad?' O'Toole said, when he perceived that she was crying.

'I'll give you two seconds,' Eithne warned, as she held the flower-pot high, ready to throw it at O'Toole's stupefied face.

'You're a nice bunch of hard-faced aul crows, crows,' he said. 'Wouldn't give a man a squeeze,' and he went out cursing each one of them. They shut the door very quickly and dragged the sideboard in front of the door so that he could not break in when they were asleep.

They got into bed in their underwear; Mary and Eithne at one end with Crystal's feet between their faces.

'You have lovely hair,' Eithne whispered to Mary. It was the nicest thing she could think of to say. They each said their prayers, and shook hands under the covers and settled down to sleep.

'Hey,' Doris O'Beirne said a few seconds later, 'I never went to the lav.'

'You can't go now,' Eithne said, 'the sideboard's in front of the door.'

'I'll die if I don't go,' Doris O'Beirne said.

'And me, too, after all that orange we drank,' Crystal said. Mary was shocked that they could talk like that. At home you never spoke of such a thing, you just went out behind the hedge and that was that. Once a work-man saw her squatting down and from that day she never talked to him, or acknowledged that she knew him.

'Maybe we could use that old pot,' Doris O'Beirne said, and Eithne Duggan sat up and said that if anyone used a pot in that room she wasn't going to sleep there.

'We have to use something,' Doris said. By now she had got up and had switched on the light. She held the pot up to the naked bulb and saw what looked to be a hole in it.

'Try it,' Crystal said, giggling.

They heard feet on the landing and then the sound of choking and coughing, and later O'Toole cursing and swearing and hitting the wall with his fist. Mary curled down under the clothes, thankful for the company of the girls. They stopped talking.

'I was at a party. Now I know what parties are like,' Mary said to herself, as she tried to force herself asleep. She heard a sound as of water running, but it did not seem to be raining outside. Later, she dozed, but at daybreak she heard the hall door bang, and she sat up in bed abruptly. She had to be home early to milk, so she got up, took her shoes and her lace dress, and let herself out by dragging the sideboard forward, and opening the door slightly.

There were newspapers spread on the landing floor and in the lavatory, and a heavy smell pervaded. Down-stairs, porter had flowed out of the bar into the hall. It was probably O'Toole who had turned on the taps of the five porter barrels, and the stone-floored bar and sunken passage outside was swimming with black porter. Mrs Rodgers would kill somebody. Mary put on her high-heeled shoes and picked her steps carefully across the room to the door. She left without even making a cup of tea.

She wheeled her bicycle down the alley and into the street. The front tyre was dead flat. She pumped for a half-an-hour but it remained flat.

The frost lay like a spell upon the street, upon the sleeping windows, and the slate roofs of the narrow houses. It had magically made the dunged street white and clean. She did not feel tired, but relieved to be out, and stunned by lack of sleep she inhaled the beauty of the morning. She walked briskly, sometimes looking back to see the track which her bicycle and her feet made on the white road.

Mrs Rodgers wakened at eight and stumbled out in her big nightgown from Brogan's warm bed. She smelt disaster instantly and hurried downstairs to find the porter in the bar and the hall; then she ran to call the others.

'Porter all over the place; every drop of drink in the house is on the floor – Mary Mother of God help me in my tribulation! Get up, get up.' She rapped on their door and called the girls by name.

The girls rubbed their sleepy eyes, yawned, and sat up.

'She's gone,' Eithne said, looking at the place on the pillow where Mary's head had been.

'Oh, a sneaky country one,' Doris said, as she got into her taffeta dress and went down to see the flood. 'If I have to clean that, in my good clothes, I'll die,' she said. But Mrs Rodgers had already brought brushes and pails and got to work. They opened the bar door and began to bail the porter into the street. Dogs came to lap it up, and Hickey, who had by then come down, stood and said what a crying shame it was, to waste all that drink. Outside it washed away an area of frost and revealed the dung of yesterday's fair day. O'Toole the culprit had fled since the night; Long John Salmon was gone for his swim, and upstairs in bed Brogan snuggled down for a last-minute warm and deliberated on the joys that he would miss when he left the Commercial for good.

'And where's my lady with the lace dress?' Hickey asked, recalling very little of Mary's face, but distinctly remembering the sleeves of her black dress which dipped into the plates.

'Sneaked off, before we were up,' Doris said. They all agreed that Mary was no bloody use and should never have been asked.

'And 'twas she set O'Toole mad, egging him on and then disappointing him,' Doris said, and Mrs Rodgers swore that O'Toole, or Mary's father, or someone, would pay dear for the wasted drink.

'I suppose she's home by now,' Hickey said, as he rooted in his pocket for a butt. He had a new packet, but if he produced that they'd all be puffing away at his expense.

Mary was half-a-mile from home, sitting on a bank.

If only I had a sweetheart, something to hold on to, she thought, as she cracked some ice with her high heel and watched the crazy splintered pattern it made. The poor birds could get no food as the ground was frozen hard. Frost was general all over Ireland; frost like a weird blossom on the branches, on the river-bank from which Long John Salmon leaped in his great, hairy nakedness, on the ploughs left out all winter; frost on the stony fields, and on all the slime and ugliness of the world.

Walking again she wondered if and what she would tell her mother and her brothers about it, and if all parties were as bad. She was at the top of the hill now, and could see her own house, like a little white box at the end of the world, waiting to receive her.

Cords

Everything was ready, the suitcase closed, her black velvet coat-collar carefully brushed, and a list pinned to the wall reminding her husband when to feed the hens and turkeys, and what foodstuffs to give them. She was setting out on a visit to her daughter Claire in London, just like any mother, except that *her* daughter was different: she'd lost her faith, and she mixed with queer people and wrote poems. If it was stories one could detect the sin in them, but these poems made no sense at all and therefore seemed more wicked. Her daughter had sent the money for the air-ticket. She was going now, kissing her husband good-bye, tender towards him in a way that she never was, throughout each day, as he spent his time looking through the window at the wet currant bushes, grumbling about the rain, but was in fact pleased at the excuse to hatch indoors, and asked for tea all the time, which he lapped from a saucer, because it was more pleasurable.

'The turkeys are the most important,' she said, kissing him good-bye, and thinking faraway to the following Christmas, to the turkeys she would sell, and the plumper ones she would give as gifts.

'I hope you have a safe flight,' he said. She'd never flown before.

'All Irish planes are blessed, they never crash,' she

said, believing totally in the God that created her, sent her this venial husband, a largish farmhouse, hens, hardship, and one daughter who'd changed, become moody, and grown away from them completely.

The journey was pleasant once she'd got over the shock of being strapped down for the take-off. As they went higher and higher she looked out at the very white, wispish cloud and thought of the wash tub and hoped her husband would remember to change his shirt while she was away. The trip would have been perfect but that there was a screaming woman who had to be calmed down by the air hostess. She looked like a woman who was being sent to a mental institution, but did not know it.

Claire met her mother at the airport and they kissed warmly, not having seen each other for over a year.

'Have you stones in it?' Claire said, taking the fibre suitcase. It was doubly secured with a new piece of binding twine. Her mother wore a black straw hat with clusters of cherries on both sides of the brim.

'You were great to meet me,' the mother said.

'Of course I'd meet you,' Claire said, easing her mother right back on the taxi seat. It was a long ride and they might as well be comfortable.

'I could have navigated,' the mother said, and Claire said nonsense a little too brusquely. Then to make amends she asked gently how the journey was.

'Oh I must tell you, there was this very peculiar woman and she was screaming.'

Claire listened and stiffened, remembering her mother's voice that became low and dramatic in a crisis, the same voice that said, 'Sweet Lord your father will kill us', or, 'What's to become of us, the bailiff is here', or, 'Look, look, the chimney is on fire.'

'But otherwise?' Claire said. This was a holiday, not an expedition into the past.

'We had tea and sandwiches. I couldn't eat mine, the bread was buttered.'

'Still faddy?' Claire said. Her mother got bilious if she touched butter, fish, olive oil, or eggs; although her daily diet was mutton stew, or home-cured bacon.

'Anyhow, I have nice things for you,' Claire said. She had bought in stocks of biscuits, jellies and preserves because these were the things her mother favoured, these foods that she herself found distasteful.

The first evening passed well enough. The mother unpacked the presents – a chicken, bread, eggs, a tapestry of a church spire which she'd done all winter, stitching at it until she was almost blind, a holy water font, ashtrays made from shells, lamps converted from bottles, and a picture of a matador assembled by sticking small varnished pebbles on to hardboard.

Claire laid them along the mantelshelf in the kitchen, and stood back, not so much to admire them as to see how incongruous they looked, piled together.

'Thank you,' she said to her mother, as tenderly as she might have when she was a child. These gifts touched her, especially the tapestry, although it was ugly. She thought of the winter nights and the Aladdin lamp smoking (they expected the electricity to be installed soon), and her mother hunched over her work, not even using a thimble to ease the needle through, because she believed in sacrifice, and her father turning to say, 'Could I borrow your glasses, Mam, I want to have a look at the paper?' He was too lazy to have his own eyes tested and believed that his wife's glasses were just as good. She could picture them at the fire night after night, the turf flames green and fitful, the hens locked up, foxes prowling around in the wind, outside.

'I'm glad you like it, I did it specially for you,' the mother said gravely, and they both stood with tears in their eyes, savouring those seconds of tenderness, knowing that it would be short-lived.

'You'll stay seventeen days,' Claire said, because that was the length an economy ticket allowed. She really meant, 'Are you staying seventeen days?'

'If it's all right,' her mother said over-humbly. 'I don't see you that often, and I miss you.'

Claire withdrew into the scullery to put on the kettle for her mother's hot water bottle; she did not want any disclosures now, any declaration about how hard life had been and how near they'd been to death during many of the father's drinking deliriums.

'Your father sent you his love,' her mother said, nettled because Claire had not asked how he was.

'How is he?'

'He's great now, never touches a drop.'

Claire knew that if he had, he would have descended on her, the way he used to descend on her as a child when she was in the convent, or else she would have had a telegram, of clipped urgency, 'Come home. Mother.'

'It was God did it, curing him like that,' the mother said.

Claire thought bitterly that God had taken too long to help the thin frustrated man who was emaciated, crazed and bankrupted by drink. But she said nothing, she merely filled the rubber bottle, pressed the air from it with her arm, and then conducted her mother upstairs to bed.

Next morning they went up to the centre of London

and Claire presented her mother with fifty pounds. The woman got flushed and began to shake her head, the quick uncontrolled movements resembling those of a beast with the staggers.

'You always had a good heart, too good,' she said to her daughter, as her eyes beheld racks of coats, raincoats, skirts on spinning hangers, and all kinds and colours of hats.

'Try some on,' Claire said. 'I have to make a phone call.'

There were guests due to visit her that night – it had been arranged weeks before – but as they were bohemian people, she could not see her mother suffering them, or them suffering her mother. There was the added complication that they were a 'trio' – one man and two women; his wife and his mistress. At that point in their lives the wife was noticeably pregnant.

On the telephone the mistress said they were looking forward, awfully, to the night, and Claire heard herself substantiate the invitation by saying she had simply rung up to remind them. She thought of asking another man to give a complexion of decency to the evening, but the only three unattached men she could think of had been lovers of hers and she could not call on them; it seemed pathetic.

'Damn,' she said, irritated by many things, but mainly by the fact that she was going through one of those bleak, loveless patches that come in everyone's life, but, she imagined, came more frequently the older one got. She was twenty-eight. Soon she would be thirty. Withering.

'How do?' her mother said in a ridiculous voice when Claire returned. She was holding a hand mirror

up to get a back view of a ridiculous hat, which she
had tried on. It resembled the shiny straw she wore
for her trip, except that it was more ornamental and
cost ten guineas. That was the second point about it
that Claire noted. The white price tag was hanging
over the mother's nose. Claire hated shopping the way
other people might hate going to the dentist. For herself she never shopped. She merely saw things in windows, ascertained the size, and bought them.

'Am I too old for it?' the mother said. A loaded question in itself.

'You're not,' Claire said. 'You look well in it.'

'Of course I've always loved hats,' her mother said, as
if admitting to some secret vice. Claire remembered
drawers with felt hats laid into them, and bobbins on
the brims of hats, and little aprons of veiling, with
spots which, as a child, she thought might crawl over
the wearer's face.

'Yes, I remember your hats,' Claire said, remembering too the smell of empty perfume bottles and cam-
phor, and a saxe-blue hat that her mother once got on
approbation, by post, and wore to Mass before returning it to the shop.

'If you like it, take it,' Claire said indulgently.

The mother bought it, along with a reversible raincoat and a pair of shoes. She told the assistant who
measured her feet about a pair of shoes which lasted
her for seventeen years, and were eventually stolen by
a tinker-woman, who afterwards was sent to jail for the
theft.

'Poor old creature I wouldn't have wished jail on
her,' the mother said, and Claire nudged her to shut
up. The mother's face flushed under the shelter of her
new, wide-brimmed hat.

'Did I say something wrong?' she said as she descended uneasily on the escalator, her parcels held close to her.

'No, I just thought she was busy, it isn't like shops at home,' Claire said.

'I think she was enjoying the story,' her mother said, gathering courage before she stepped off, on to the ground floor.

At home they prepared the food and the mother tidied the front room before the visitors arrived. Without a word she carried all her own trophies – the tapestry, the pebble picture, the ashtrays, the holy water font and the other ornaments – and put them in the front room alongside the books, the pencil drawings and the poster of Bengal that was a left-over from Claire's dark-skinned lover.

'They're nicer in here,' the mother said, apologizing for doing it, and at the same time criticizing the drawing of the nude.

'I'd get rid of some of those things if I were you,' she said in a serious tone to her daughter.

Claire kept silent, and sipped the whisky she felt she needed badly. Then to get off the subject she asked after her mother's feet. They were fixing a chiropodist appointment for the next day.

The mother had changed into a blue blouse, Claire into velvet pants, and they sat before the fire on low pouffes with a blue-shaded lamp casting a restful light on their very similar faces. At sixty, and made-up, the mother still had a poem of a face: round, pale, perfect and with soft eyes, expectant, in spite of what life had brought. On the whites there had appeared blobs of green, the sad green of old age.

'You have a tea-leaf on your eyelid,' she said to Claire, putting up her hand to brush it away. It was mascara which got so smeared that Claire had to go upstairs to repair it.

At that precise moment the visitors came.

'They're here,' the mother said when the hall bell shrieked.

'Open the door,' Claire called down.

'Won't it look odd, if you don't do it?' the mother said.

'Oh, open it,' Claire called impatiently. She was quite relieved that they would have to muddle through their own set of introductions.

The dinner went off well. They all liked the food and the mother was not as shy as Claire expected. She told about her journey, but kept the 'mad woman' episode out of it, and about a television programme she'd once seen, showing how bird's nest soup was collected. Only her voice was unnatural.

After dinner Claire gave her guests enormous brandies, because she felt relieved that nothing disastrous had been uttered. Her mother never drank spirits of course.

The fulfilled guests sat back, sniffed brandy, drank their coffee, laughed, tipped their cigarette ash on the floor, having missed the ashtray by a hair's breadth, gossiped, and re-filled their glasses. They smiled at the various new ornaments but did not comment, except to say that the tapestry was nice.

'Claire likes it,' the mother said timidly, drawing them into another silence. The evening was punctuated by brief but crushing silences.

'You like Chinese food then?' the husband said. He mentioned a restaurant which she ought to go and see.

It was in the East End of London and getting there entailed having a motor-car.

'You've been there?' his wife said to the young blonde mistress who had hardly spoken.

'Yes and it was super except for the pork which was drowned in Chanel Number Five. Remember?' she said, turning to the husband, who nodded.

'We must go some time,' his wife said. 'If ever you can spare an evening.' She was staring at the big brandy snifter that she let rock back and forth in her lap. It was for rose petals but when she saw it she insisted on drinking from it. The petals were already dying on the mantelshelf.

'That was the night we found a man against a wall, beaten up,' the mistress said, shivering, recalling how she had actually shivered.

'You were so sorry for him,' the husband said, amused.

'Wouldn't anyone be?' the wife said tartly, and Claire turned to her mother and promised that they would go to that restaurant the following evening.

'We'll see,' the mother said. She knew the places she wanted to visit: Buckingham Palace, the tower of London and the waxworks museum. When she went home it was these places she would discuss with her neighbours who'd already been to London, not some seamy place where men were flung against walls.

'No, not another, it's not good for the baby,' the husband said, as his wife balanced her empty glass on the palm of her hand and looked towards the bottle.

'Who's the more important, me or the baby?'

'Don't be silly, Marigold,' the husband said.

'Excuse me,' she said in a changed voice. 'Whose welfare are you thinking about?' She was on the verge of an emotional outburst, her cheeks flushed from brandy and umbrage. By contrast Claire's mother had the appearance of a tombstone, chalk white and deadly still.

'How is the fire?' Claire said, staring at it. On that cue her mother jumped up and sailed off with the coal scuttle.

'I'll get it,' Claire said following. The mother did not even wait until they reached the kitchen.

'Tell me,' she said, her blue eyes pierced with insult, 'which of those two ladies is he married to?'

'It's not your concern,' Claire said, hastily. She had meant to smooth it over, to say that the pregnant woman had some mental disturbance, but instead she said hurtful things about her mother being narrow-minded and cruel.

'Show me your friends and I know who you are,' the mother said and went away to shovel the coal. She left the filled bucket outside the living-room door and went upstairs. Claire, who had gone back to her guests, heard the mother's footsteps climbing the stairs and going into the bedroom overhead.

'Is your mother gone to bed?' the husband asked.

'She's tired I expect,' Claire said, conveying weariness too. She wanted them to go. She could not confide in them even though they were old friends. They might sneer. They were not friends any more than the ex-lovers, they were all social appendages, extras, acquaintances cultivated in order to be able to say to other acquaintances, 'Well one night a bunch of us went mad and had a nude sit-in . . .' There was no one she trusted, no one she could produce for her mother and feel happy about it.

'Music, brandy, cigarettes . . .' They were recalling

her, voicing their needs, wondering who would go to the machine for the cigarettes. Pauline did. They stayed until they'd finished the packet, which was well after midnight.

Claire hurried to her mother's room and found her awake with the light on, fingering her horn rosary beads. The same old black ones.

'I'm sorry,' Claire said.

'You turned on me like a tinker,' her mother said, in a voice cracked with emotion.

'I didn't mean to,' Claire said. She tried to sound reasonable, assured; she tried to tell her mother that the world was a big place and contained many people, all of whom held various views about various things.

'They're not sincere,' her mother said, stressing the last word.

'And who is?' Claire said, remembering the treacherous way the lovers vanished, or how former landladies rigged meters so that units of electricity cost double. Her mother had no notion of how lonely it was to read manuscripts all day, and write a poem once in a while, when one became consumed with a memory or an idea, and then to constantly go out, seeking people, hoping that one of them might fit, might know the shorthand of her, body and soul.

'I was a good mother, I did everything I could, and this is all the thanks I get.' It was spoken with such justification that Claire turned and laughed, hysterically. An incident leaped to her tongue, something she had never recalled before.

'You went to hospital,' she said to her mother, 'to have your toe lanced, and you came home and told me, *me*, that the doctor said, "Raise your right arm until I give you an injection", but when you did, he gave you no injection, he just cut into your toe. Why did you tell it?' The words fell out of her mouth unexpectedly, and she became aware of the awfulness when she felt her knees shaking.

'What are you talking about?' her mother said numbly. The face that was round, in the evening, had become old, twisted, bitter.

'Nothing,' Claire said. Impossible to explain. She had violated all the rules: decency, kindness, caution. She would never be able to laugh it off in the morning. Muttering an apology she went to her own room and sat on her bed, trembling. Since her mother's arrival every detail of her childhood kept dogging her. Her present life, her work, the friends she had, seemed insubstantial compared with all that had happened before. She could count the various batches of white, hissing geese – it was geese in those days – that wandered over the swampy fields, one year after another, hid in memory she could locate the pot-holes on the driveway where rain lodged, and where leaking oil from a passing car made rainbows. Looking down into rainbows to escape the colour that was in her mind, or on her tongue. She'd licked four fingers once that were slit by an unexpected razor blade which was wedged upright in a shelf where she'd reached to find a sweet, or to finger the secret dust up there. The same colour had been on her mother's violated toe underneath the big, bulky bandage. In chapel too, the sanctuary light was a bowl of blood with a flame laid into it. These images did not distress her at the time. She used to love to slip into the chapel, alone, in the daytime, moving from one Station of the Cross to the next, being God's exclusive pet, praying that she would die before her mother did, in order to escape being the scapegoat of her father. How could she have known, how could any of them have known that twenty years later, zipped into a heated, plastic tent, treating herself to a steam bath she would suddenly panic and cry out convinced that her sweat became as drops of blood. She put her hands through the flaps and begged the masseuse to protect her, the way she had begged her mother, long ago. Made a fool of herself. The way she made a fool of herself with the various men. The first night she met the Indian she was wearing a white fox collar, and its whiteness under his dark, well-chiselled chin made a stark sight as they walked through a mirrored room to a table, and saw, and were seen in mirrors. He said something she couldn't hear.

'Tell me later,' she said, already putting her little claim on him, already saying, 'You are not going to abandon me in this room of mirrors, in my bluish-white fox that so compliments your bluish-black lips.' But after a few weeks he left, like the others. She was familiar with the various tactics of withdrawal — abrupt, honest, nice. Flowers, notes posted from the provinces, and the 'I don't want you to get hurt' refrain. They reminded her of the trails that slugs leave on a lawn in summer mornings, the sad, silver trails of departure. Their goings were far more vivid than their comings, or was she only capable of remembering the worst? Remembering everything, solving nothing. She undressed, she told herself that her four fingers had healed, that her mother's big toe was now like any other person's big toe, that her father drank tea and held his temper, and that one day she would meet a man whom she loved and did not frighten away. But it was brandy optimism. She'd gone down and carried the bottle up. The brandy gave her hope but it disturbed her heart beats and she was unable to sleep. As morning approached she rehearsed the sweet and conciliatory things she would say to her mother.

They went to Mass on Sunday, but it was obvious that Claire was not in the habit of going: they had to ask the way. Going in, her mother took a small liqueur bottle from her handbag and filled it with holy water from the font.

'It's always good to have it,' she said to Claire, but in a bashful way. The outburst had severed them, and they were polite now in a way that should never have been.

After Mass they went – because the mother had stated her wishes – to the waxworks museum, saw the Tower of London and walked across the park that faced Buckingham Palace.

'Very good grazing here,' the mother said. Her new shoes were getting spotted from the damp, highish grass. It was raining. The spokes of the mother's umbrella kept tapping Claire's, and no matter how far she drew away, the mother moved accordingly, to prong her, it seemed.

'You know,' the mother said. 'I was thinking.'

Claire knew what was coming. Her mother wanted to go home; she was worried about her husband, her fowls, the washing that would have piled up, the spring wheat that would have to be sown. In reality she was miserable. She and her daughter were farther away now than when they wrote letters each week and discussed the weather, or work, or the colds they'd had.

'You're only here six days,' Claire said, 'And I want to take you to the theatre and restaurants. Don't go.'

'I'll think about it,' the mother said. But her mind was made up.

Two evenings later they waited in the airport lounge,

hesitant to speak, for fear they might miss the flight number.

'The change did you good,' Claire said. Her mother was togged out in new clothes and looked smarter. She had two more new hats in her hand, carrying them in the hope they would escape the notice of the customs men.

'I'll let you know if I have to pay duty on them,' she said.

'Do,' Claire said, smiling, straightening her mother's collar, wanting to say something endearing, something that would atone, without having to go over their differences, word for word.

'No one can say but that you fitted me out well, look at all my style,' the mother said smiling at her image in the glass door of the telephone box. 'And our trip up the river,' she said. 'I think I enjoyed it more than anything.' She was referring to a short trip they'd taken down the Thames to Westminster. They had planned to go in the opposite direction towards the greenness of Kew and Hampton Court but they'd left it – at least Claire had left it – too late and could only go towards the city on a passenger boat that was returning from those green places.

Claire had been miserly with her time and on that particular evening she'd sat at her desk pretending to work, postponing the time until she got up and rejoined her mother, who was downstairs sewing on all the buttons that had fallen off over the years. And now the mother was thanking her, saying it had been lovely. Lovely. They had passed warehouses and cranes brought to their evening standstill yellow and tilted, pylons like floodlit honeycombs in the sky, and boats, and gasworks, and filthy chimneys. The spring evening had been drenched with sewerage smell and yet her mother went on being thankful.

'I hope my mad lady won't be aboard,' the mother said, trying to make a joke out of it now.

'Not likely,' Claire said, but the mother declared that life was full of strange and sad coincidences. They looked at each other, looked away, criticized a man who was wolfing sandwiches from his pocket, looked at the airport clock and compared the time on their watches.

'Sssh ... sssh ...' Claire had to say.

'That's it,' they both said then, relieved. As if they had secretly feared the flight number would never be called.

At the barrier they kissed, their damp cheeks touched and stayed for a second like that, each registering the other's sorrow.

'I'll write to you, I'll write oftener,' Claire said, and for a few minutes she stood there waving, weeping, not aware that the visit was over and that she could go back to her own life now, such as it was.

Paradise

In the harbour were the four boats. A boat named after a country, a railroad, an emotion and a girl. She first saw them at sundown. Very beautiful they were and tranquil, white boats at a distance from each other, cosseting the harbour. On the far side a mountain. Lilac at that moment. It seemed to be made of collapsible substance so insubstantial was it. Between the boats and the mountain a lighthouse, on an island.

Somebody said the light was not nearly so pretty as in the old days when the coastguard lived there and worked it by gas. It was automatic now and much brighter. Between them and the sea were four fields cultivated with fig trees. Dry yellow fields that seemed to be exhaling dust. No grass. She looked again at the four boats, the fields, the fig trees, the suave ocean, she looked at the house behind her and she thought, It can be mine, mine, and her heart gave a little somersault. He recognized her agitation and smiled. The house acted like a spell on all who came. He took her by the hand and led her up the main stairs. Stone stairs with a wobbly banister. The undersides of each step bright blue. 'Stop,' he said, where it got dark near the top, and before he switched on the light.

A servant had unpacked for her. There were flowers in the room. They smelt of confectionery. In the bath-

room a great glass urn filled with talcum powder. She
leaned over the rim and inhaled. It caused her to sneeze
three times. Ovaries of dark-purple soap had been
taken out of their wrapping paper and for several
minutes she held one in either hand. Yes. She had done
the right thing in coming. She need not have feared,
he needed her, his expression and their clasped hands
already confirmed that.

They sat on the terrace drinking a cocktail he had
made. It was of rum and lemon and proved to be
extremely potent. One of the guests said the angle of
light on the mountain was at its most magnificent.
He put his fingers to his lips and blew a kiss to the
mountain. She counted the peaks, thirteen in all,
with a plateau between the first four and the last
nine.

The peaks were close to the sky. Farther down on
the face of the mountain various juts stuck out, and
these made shadows on their neighbouring juts. She
was told its name. At the same moment she overheard
a question being put to a young woman, 'Are you in-
terested in Mary Queen of Scots?' The woman whose
skin had a beguiling radiance answered yes over-
readily. It was possible that such a radiance was the
result of constant supplies of male sperm. The man
had a high pale forehead and a look of death.

They drank. They smoked. All twelve smokers toss-
ing the butts on to the tiled roof that sloped towards
the farm buildings. Summer lightning started up. It
was random and quiet and faintly theatrical. It seemed
to be something devised for their amusement. It lit one
part of the sky, then another. There were bats flying
about also, and their dark shapes and the random

gentle shots of summer lightning were a distraction, and gave them something to point to. 'If I had a horse I'd call it Summer Lightning,' one of the women said, and the man next to her said how charming. She knew she ought to speak. She wanted to. Both for his sake and for her own. Her mind would give a little leap and be still and would leap again, words were struggling to be set free, to say something, a little amusing something to establish her among them. But her tongue was tied. They would know her predecessors. They would compare her minutely, her appearance, her accent, the way he behaved with her. They would know better than she how important she was to him, if it were serious or just a passing notion. They had all read in the gossip columns how she came to meet him; how he had gone to have an X-ray and met her there, the radiographer in white, committed to a dark room and films showing lungs and pulmonary tracts.

'Am I right in thinking you are to take swimming lessons?' a man asked, choosing the moment when she had leaned right back and was staring up at a big pine tree.

'Yes,' she said, wishing that he had not been told.

'There's nothing to it, you just get in and swim,' he said.

How surprised they all were, surprised and amused. Asked where she had lived and if it were really true.

'Can't imagine anyone not swimming as a child.'

'Can't imagine anyone not swimming, period.'

'Nothing to it, you just fight, fight.'

The sun filtered by the green needles fell and made play on the dense clusters of brown nuts. They never ridicule nature, she thought, they never dare. He came and stood behind her, his hand patting her bare pale shoulder. A man who was not holding a camera pretended to take a photograph of them. How long would she last, It would be uppermost in all their minds.

'We'll take you on the boat tomorrow,' he said. They cooed. They all went to such pains, such excesses to describe the cruiser. They competed with each other to tell her. They were really telling him. She thought I should be honest, say I do not like the sea, say I am an inland person, that I like rain and roses in a field, thin rain and through it the roses and the vegetation, and that my sea is dark as the shells of mussels, and signifies catastrophe. But she couldn't.

'It must be wonderful,' was what she said.

'It's quite, quite something,' he said, shyly.

At dinner she sat at one end of the egg-shaped table and he at the other. Six white candles in glass sconces separated them. The secretary had arranged the places. A fat woman on his right wore a lot of silver bracelets and was veiled in crêpe. They had cold soup to start with. The garnishings were so finely chopped that it was impossible to identify each one except by its flavour. She slipped out of her shoes. A man describing his trip to India dwelt for an unnaturally long time on the disgustingness of the food. He had gone to see the temples. Another man, who was repeatedly trying to buoy them up, threw the question to the table at large: 'Which of the Mediterranean ports is best to dock at?' Everyone had a favourite. Some picked ports where exciting things had happened, some chose ports where the approach was most beguiling, harbour fees were compared as a matter of interest; the man who had asked the question amused them all with an account of a cruise he had made once with his young daughter and of how he was unable to land when they got to Venice because of inebriation. She had to admit that she did not know enough ports. They were touched by that confession.

'We're going to try them all,' he said from the opposite end of the table, 'and keep a log book.' People looked from him to her and smiled, knowingly.

That night behind closed shutters they enacted their rite. They were both impatient to get there. Long before the coffee had been brought they had moved away from the table and contrived to be alone, choosing the stone seat that girdled the big pine tree. The seat was smeared all over with the tree's transparent gum. The nuts bobbing together made a dull clatter as of castanets. They sat for as long as courtesy required, then they retired. In bed she felt safe again, united to him not only by passion and by pleasure but by some more radical entanglement. She had no name for it, that puzzling emotion that was more than love, or perhaps less, that was not simply sexual although sex was vital to it and held it together like wires supporting a broken bowl. They both had had many breakages and therefore loved with a wary superstition.

'What you do to me,' he said. 'How you know me, all my vibrations.'

'I think we are connected underneath,' she said, quietly. She often thought he hated her for implicating him in something too tender. But he was not hating her then.

At length it was necessary to go back to her bedroom because he had promised to get up early to go spearfishing with the men.

As she kissed him good-bye she caught sight of herself in the chrome surface of the coffee flask which was on his bedside table – eyes emitting satisfaction and chagrin and panic were what stared back at her. Each time as she left him she expected not to see him again; each parting promised to be final.

The men left soon after six, she heard car doors because she had been unable to sleep.

In the morning she had her first swimming lesson. It was arranged that she would take it when the others sat down to breakfast. Her instructor had been brought from England. She asked if he'd slept well. She did not ask where. The servants disappeared from the house late at night and departed towards the settlement of low-roofed buildings. The dog went with them. The instructor told her to go backwards down the metal step ladder. There were wasps hovering about and she thought that if she were to get stung she could by-pass the lesson. No wasp obliged.

Some children who had been swimming earlier had left their plastic toys – a yellow ring that craned into the neck and head of a duck. It was a duck with a thoroughly disgusted expression. There was as well a blue dolphin with a name painted on it and all kinds of battleships. They were the children of guests. The older ones, who were boys, took no notice of any of the adults and moved about, raucous and meddlesome, taking full advantage of every aspect of the place – at night they watched the lizards patiently and for hours, in the heat of the day they remained in the water, in the early morning they gathered almonds for which they received from him a harvesting fee. One black flipper lurked on the floor of the pool. She looked down at it and touched it with her toe. Those were her last unclaimed moments, those moments before the lesson began.

The instructor told her to sit, to sit in it, as if it were a bath. He crouched and slowly she crouched too. 'Now hold your nose and put your head under water,' he said. She pulled the bathing cap well over her ears and forehead to protect her hair-style and with her nose gripped too tightly she went underneath. 'Feel it?' he said excitedly. 'Feel the water holding you up?' She felt no such thing. She felt the water smothering her. He told her to press the water from her eyes. He was gentleness itself. Then he dived in, swam a few strokes and stood up shaking the water from his grey hair. He took her hands, and walked backwards until they were at arm's length. He asked her to lie on her stomach and give herself to it. He promised not to let go of her hands. Each time on the verge of doing so she stopped: first her body, then her mind refused. She felt that if she were to take her feet off the ground the unmentionable would happen. 'What do I fear?' she asked herself. 'Death,' she said, and yet it was not that. It was as if some horrible experiences would happen before her actual death. She thought perhaps it might be the fight she would put up.

When she succeeded in stretching out for one desperate minute he proclaimed with joy. But that first lesson was a failure as far as she was concerned. Walking back to the house she realized it was a mistake to have allowed an instructor to be brought. It put too much emphasis on it. It would be incumbent upon her to conquer it. They would concern themselves with her progress, not because they cared, but like the summer lightning or the yachts going by it would be something to talk about. But she could not send the instructor home. He was an old man and he had never been abroad before. Already he was marvelling at the scenery. She had to go on with it. Going back to the terrace she was not sure of her feet on land, she was not sure of land itself; it seemed to sway, and her knees shook uncontrollably.

When she sat down to breakfast she found that a saucer of almonds had been peeled for her. They were sweet and fresh, re-invoking the sweetness and freshness of a country morning. They tasted like hazel nuts. She said so. Nobody agreed. Nobody disagreed. Some were reading papers. Now and then someone read a piece aloud, some amusing piece about some acquaintance of theirs who had done a dizzy newsworthy thing. The children read the thermometer and argued about the pencilled shadow on the sun dial. The temperature was already in the eighties. The women were forming a plan to go on the speedboat to get their midriffs brown. She declined. He called her into the conservatory and said she might give some time to supervising the meals because the secretary had rather a lot to do.

Passion flower leaves were stretched along the roof on lifelines of green cord. Each leaf like the five fingers of a hand. Green and yellow leaves on the same hand. No flowers. Flowers later. Flowers that would live a day. Or so the gardener had said. She said, 'I hope we will be here to see one.' 'If you want, we will,' he said, but of course he might take a notion and go. He never knew what he might do, no one knew.

When she entered the vast kitchen the first thing the servants did was to smile. Women in black, with soft-

soled shoes, all smiling, no complicity in any of those
smiles. She had brought with her a phrase book, a
notebook and an English cookery book. The kitchen
was like a laboratory—various white machines stationed
against the walls, refrigerators churtling at different
speeds, a fan over each of the electric cookers, the red
and green lights on the dials faintly menacing as if
they were about to issue an alarm. There was a huge
fish on the table. It had been speared that morning by
the men. Its mouth was open; its eyes so close
together that they barely missed being one eye; its
lower lip gaped pathetically. The fins were black and
matted with oil. They all stood and looked at it, she
and the seven or eight willing women to whom she
must make herself understood. When she sat to copy
the recipe from the English book and translate it
into their language they turned on another fan.
Already they were chopping for the evening meal.
Three young girls chopped onions, tomatoes and
peppers. They seemed to take pleasure in their tasks,
they seemed to smile into the mounds of vegetable that
they so diligently chopped.

There were eight picnic baskets to be taken on the
boat. And armfuls of towels. The children begged to
be allowed to carry the towels. He had the zip bag with
the wine bottles. He shook the bag so that the bottles
rattled in their surrounds of ice. The guests smiled. He
had a way of drawing people into his mood without
having to say or do much. Conversely he had a way
of locking people out. Both things were mesmerizing.
They crossed the four fields that led to the sea. The
figs were hard and green. The sun played like a blow-
lamp upon her back and neck. He said that she would
have to lather herself in sun-oil. It seemed oddly hostile,

his saying it out loud like that, in front of the others. As they got nearer the water she felt her heart race. The water was all shimmer. Some swam out, some got in the rowing boat. Trailing her hand in the crinkled surface of the water she thought it is not cramp, jellyfish, or broken glass that I fear, it is something else. A ladder was dropped down at the side of the boat, for the swimmers to climb in from the sea. Sandals had to be kicked off as they stepped inside. The floor was of blond wood and burning hot. Swimmers had to have their feet inspected for tar marks. The boatman stood with a pad of cotton soaked in petrol ready to rub the marks. The men busied themselves – one helped to get the engine going, a couple put awnings up, others carried out large striped cushions, and scattered them under the awnings. Two boys refused to come on board.

'It is pleasant to bash my little brother up under water,' a young boy said, his voice at once menacing and melodious.

She smiled and went down steps where there was a kitchen, and sleeping quarters with beds for four. He followed her. He looked, inhaled deeply and murmured.

'Take it out,' she said, 'I want it now, now.' Timorous and whim mad. How he loved it. How he loved that imperative. He pushed the door and she watched as he struggled to take down the shorts, but could not get the cord undone. He was the awkward one now. How he stumbled. She waited for one excruciating moment and made him wait. Then she knelt and as she began he muttered between clenched teeth. He who could tame animals was defenceless in this. She applied herself to it, sucking, sucking, sucking with all the hunger that

she felt and all the simulated hunger that she liked
him to think she felt. Threatening to maim him she
always just grazed with the edges of her fine square
teeth. Nobody intruded. It took no more than minutes.
She stayed behind for a decent interval. She felt thirsty.
In the window ledge there were paperback books and
bottles of sun-oil. Also a spare pair of shorts that had
the names of all the likely things in the world printed
on them – the names of drinks and capital cities and
the flags of each nation. The sea through the porthole
was a small, harmless globule of blue.

They passed out of the harbour, away from the three
other boats and the settlement of pines. Soon there was
only sea and rock, no reedy inlets, no towns. Mile after
mile of hallucinating sea. The madness of mariners
conveyed itself to her, the illusion that it was land, and
that she could traverse it. A land that led to nowhere.
The rocks had been reduced to every shape that the
eye and the mind could comprehend. Near the water
there were openings that had been forced through by
the sea – some rapacious, some large enough for a small
boat to slink in under, some as small and unsettling as
the sockets of eyes. The trees on the sheer faces of these
rocks were no more than the struggle to be trees. Birds
could not perch there, let alone nest. She tried not to
remember the swimming lesson, to postpone remembering until the afternoon, until the next lesson.

She came out and joined them. A young girl sat at
the stern, among the cushions, playing a guitar. She
wore long silver spatula-shaped ear-rings. A self-
appointed gipsy. The children were playing 'I Spy'
but finding it hard to locate new objects. They were
confined to the things they could see around them. By
standing she found that the wind and the spray from

the water kept her cool. The mountains that were far away appeared insubstantial, but those that were near glinted when the sharp stones were favoured by the sun.

'I find it a little unreal,' she said to one of the men. 'Beautiful but unreal.' She had to shout because of the noise of the engine.

'I don't know what you mean by unreal,' he said.

Their repertoire was small but effective. In the intonation the sting lay. Dreadfully subtle. Impossible to bridle over. In fact the unnerving thing about it was the terrible bewilderment it induced. Was it intended or not? She distinctly remembered a sensation of once thinking that her face was laced by a cobweb but being unable to feel it with the hand and being unable to put a finger on their purulence felt exactly the same. To each other too they transmitted small malices and then moved on to the next topic. They mostly talked of places they had been to and the people who were there, and though they talked endlessly they told nothing about themselves.

They picnicked on a small pink strand. He ate very little and afterwards he walked off. She thought to follow him, then didn't. The children waded out to sea on a long whitened log and one of the women read everybody's hand. She was promised an illness. When he returned he gave his large yellowish hand reluctantly. He was promised a son. She looked at him for a gratifying sign but got none. At that moment he was telling one of the men about a black sloop that he had loved as a child. She thought, What is it that he sees in me, he who loves sea, sloops, jokes, masquerades and deferment? What is it that he sees in me who loves none of those things?

Her instructor brought flat white boards. He held
one end, she the other. She watched his hands carefully.
They were very white from being in water. She lay on
her stomach and held the boards and watched his hands
in case they should let go of the board. the boards
kept bobbing about and adding to her uncertainty. He
said a rope would be better.

The big fish had had its bones removed and was then
pieced together. A perfect decoy. Its head and its too-
near eyes were gone. On her advice the housekeeper
had taken the lemons out of the refrigerator so that
they were like lemons now rather than bits of frozen
sponge. Someone remarked on this and she felt
childishly pleased. Because of a south wind a strange
night exhilaration arose. They drank a lot. They discussed beautiful evenings. Evenings resurrected in
them by the wine and the wind and a transient good
will. One talked of watching golden cock pheasants
strutting in a backyard: one talked of bantams
perched on a gate at dusk, their forms like notes of
music on a blank bar; no one mentioned love or family,
it was scenery, or nature or a whippet that left them
with the best and most serene memories. She relived a
stormy night with an ass braying in a field and a blown
bough fallen across a road. After dinner various couples
went for walks, or swims, or to listen for children. The
three men who were single went to the village to recon-
noitre. Women confided the diets they were on, or the
face creams that they found most beneficial. A divorcée
said to her host, 'You've *got* to come to bed with me,
you've simply *got* to,' and he smiled. It was no more
than a pleasantry, another remark in a strange night's
proceedings where there were also crickets, tree frogs

143

and the sounds of clandestine kissing. The single men
came back presently and reported that the only bar was
full of Germans and that the whisky was inferior. The
one who had been most scornful about her swimming
sat at her feet and said how awfully pretty she was.
Asked her details about her life, her work, her school-
ing. Yet this friendliness only reinforced her view of
her own solitude, her apartness. She answered each
question carefully and seriously. By answering she
was subscribing to her longing to fit in. He seemed a
little jealous so she got up and went to him. He was not
really one of them either. He simply stage-managed
them for his own amusement. Away from them she
almost reached him. It was as if he were bound by a
knot, that maybe, maybe, she could unravel, for a long
stretch, living their own life, cultivating a true emotion,
independent of other people. But would they ever be
away? She dared not ask. For that kind of discussion
she had to substitute with a silence.

She stole into their rooms to find clues to their private selves – to see if they had brought sticking plaster,
indigestion pills, face flannels, the ordinary necessities.
On a dressing table there was a wig block with blonde
hair very artfully curled. On the face of the block
coloured sequins were arranged to represent the
features of an ancient Egyptian queen. The divorcée
had a baby's pillow in a yellow muslin case. Some had
carried up bottles of wine and these though not drunk
were not removed. The servants only touched what was
thrown on the floor or put in the wastepaper baskets.
Clothes for washing were thrown on the floor. It was
one of the house rules like having cocktails on the
terrace at evening time. Some had written cards which

she read eagerly. These cards told nothing except that it was all super.

His secretary, who was mousy, avoided her. Perhaps she knew too much. Plans he had made for the future.

She wrote to her doctor:

I am taking the tranquillizers but I don't feel any more relaxed. Could you send me some others?

She tore it up.

Hair got tangled by the salt in the sea air. She bought some curling tongs.

One woman, who was pregnant, kept sprinkling baby powder and smoothing it over her stomach through-out the day. They always took tea together. They were friends. She thought, If this woman were not pregnant would she be so amiable? Their kind of thinking was beginning to take root in her.

The instructor put a rope over her head. She brought it down around her middle. They heard a quack-quack. She was certain that the plastic duck had uttered. She laughed as she adjusted the noose. The instructor laughed too. He held a firm grip of the rope. She threshed through the water and tried not to think of where she was. Sometimes she did it well; some-times she had to be brought in like an old piece of lumber. She could never tell the outcome of each plunge; she never knew how it was going to be or what thoughts would suddenly obstruct her. But each time he said, 'Lovely, lovely,' and in his exuberance she found consolation.

A woman called Iris swam out to their yacht. She dangled in the water and with one hand gripped the sides of the boat. Her nail varnish was exquisitely applied and the nails had the glow of a rich imbued pearl. By contrast with the pearl coating the half-moons were chastely white. Her personality was like that too – full of glow. For each separate face she had a smile and a word or two for those she already knew. One of the men asked if she were in love. Love! She riled him. She said her good spirits were due to her breathing. She said life was a question of correct breathing. She had come to invite them for drinks but he declined because they were due back at the house. Some lawyers had been invited to lunch. She heard this without any regret and as she swam back to the shore, her poodle, who was waiting, yapped and she yapped back, mimicking its sound exactly. Those who had known her previously remarked on her new gaiety. At dinner he brought it up again. There was mention of her past escapades, the rows with her husband, his death which was thought to be a suicide and the unpleasant business of his burial which proved impossible on religious grounds. Finally his body having to be laid in a small paddock adjoining the public cemetery. Altogether an unsavoury story, yet dangling in the water had been this radiant woman with no traces of past harm.

'Yes, Iris has incredible will power, incredible,' he said.

'For what?' she asked, from the opposite end of the table.

'For living,' he said tartly.

It was not lost on others. Her jaw muscle twitched.

Again she spoke to herself, remonstrated with her hurt: 'I try, I try, I want to fit, I want to join, be the someone who slips into a crowd of marchers when the march has already begun, but there is something in me that I call sense and it baulks at your ways. It would seem as if I am here simply to smart under your strictures.' Retreating into dreams and monologue.

She posed for a picture. She posed beside the sculptured lady. She repeated the pose of the lady. Hands placed over each other and laid on the left shoulder, head inclining towards those hands. He took it. Click, click. The marble lady had been the sculptor's wife and had died tragically. The hands with their unnaturally long nail fronts were the best feature of it. Click, click. When she was not looking he took another.

She found the accounts books in a desk drawer and was surprised at the entries. Things like milk and matches had to be accounted for. She thought, Is he generous at the roots? The housekeeper had left some needlework in the book. She had old-fashioned habits and resisited much of the modern kitchen equipment. She kept the milk in little pots, with muslin spread over the top. She skimmed the cream with her fat fingers, tipped the cream into small jugs for their morning coffee. What would they say to that! In the evenings when every task was done the housekeeper sat in the back veranda with her husband, doing the mending. They had laid pine branches on the roof and these had withered, and were tough as wire. Her husband made shapes from soft pieces of new white wood, and then in the dark put his penknife aside and tickled his wife's toes. She heard them when she stole in to get some figs from the refrigerator. It was both poignant and disturbing.

The instructor let go of the rope. She panicked and stopped using her arms and legs. The water was rising up over her. The water was in complete control of her. She knew that she was screaming convulsively. He had to jump in clothes and all. Afterwards they sat in the linen room with a blanket each and drank brandy. They vouched to tell no one. The brandy went straight to his head. He said in England it would be raining and people would be queueing for buses and his eyes twinkled because of his own good fate.

More than one guest was called Teddy. One of the Teddies told her that in the mornings before his wife wakened he read Proust in the dressing-room. It enabled him to masturbate. It was no more than if he had told her he missed bacon for breakfast. For breakfast there was fruit and scrambled egg. Bacon was a rarity on the island. She said to the older children that the plastic duck was psychic and had squeaked. They laughed. Their laughing was real but they kept it up long after the joke had expired. A girl said, 'Shall I tell you a rude story?' The boys appeared to want to restrain her. The girl said, 'Once upon a time there was a lady and a blind man came to her door every evening for sixpence and one day she was in the bath and the doorbell rang and she put on a gown and came down and it was the milkman, and she got back in the bath and the doorbell rang and it was the breadman and at six o'clock the doorbell rang and she thought I don't have to put on my gown it is the blind man and when she opened the door the blind man said, "Madam, I've come to tell you I got my sight back." ' And the laughter that had never really died down started up again and the whole mountain was boisterous with it. No insect, no singing bird was heard on that walk. She had to watch the time. The children's evening meal was earlier. They ate on the back veranda and she often went there and stole a sardine or a piece of bread so as to avoid getting too drunk before dinner. There was no telling how late dinner would be. It depended on him, on whether he was bored or not. Extra guests from neighbouring houses came each evening for drinks. They added variety. The talk was about sailing and speeding, or about gardens, or about pools. They all seemed to be intrigued by these topics, even the women. One man who followed the snow knew where the best snow surfaces were for every week of every year. That subject did not bore her as much. At least the snow was nice to think about, crisp and blue like he said, and rasping under the skis. The children could often be heard shrieking but after cocktail hour they never appeared. She believed that it would be better once they were married and had children. She would be instated by courtesy of them. It was a swindle really, the fact that small creatures, ridiculously easy to beget, should solidify a relationship, but they would. Everyone hinted how he wanted a son. He was nearing sixty. She had stopped using contraceptives and he had stopped asking. Perhaps that was his way of deciding, of finally accepting her.

Gull's eggs, already shelled, were brought to table. The yolks a very delicate yellow. 'Where are the shells?' the fat lady, veiled in crêpe, asked. The shells had to be brought. They were crumbled almost to a powder but were brought anyhow. 'Where are the nests?' she asked. It missed. It was something they might have laughed at, had they heard, but a wind had risen and they were all getting up and carrying things indoors. The wind was working up to something. It whipped the geranium flowers from their leaves and crazed the candle flames so that they blew this way and that and cracked the glass sconces. That night their love-making had all the sweetness and all the release that earth must feel with the long-awaited rain. He was another man now, with another voice – loving and private and incantatory. His coldness, his dismissal of her hard to believe in. Perhaps if they quarrelled, their quarrels, like their love-making, would bring them closer. But they never did. He said he'd never had a quarrel with any of his women. She gathered that he left his wives once it got to that point. He did not say so, but she felt that must have been so, because he had once said that all his marriages were happy. He said there had been fights with men but that these were decent. He had more rapport with men; with women he was charming but it was a charm devised to keep them at bay. He had no brothers, and no son. He had had a father who bullied him and held his inheritance back for longer than he should. This she got from one of the men who had known him for forty years. His father had caused him to suffer, badly. She did not know in what way and she was unable to ask him because it was information she should never have been given a hint of.

After their trip to the Roman caves the children came home ravenous. One child objected because the meal was cold. The servant, sensing a certain levity, told her master and the story sent shrieks of laughter around the lunch table. It was repeated many times. He called to ask if she had heard. He sometimes singled her out in that way. It was one of the few times the guests could glimpse the bond between them. Yes, she had heard. 'Sweet, sweet,' she said. The word occurred in her repertoire all the time now. She was learning their language. And fawning. Far from home, from where the cattle grazed. The cattle had fields to roam, and a water tank near the house. The earth around the water tank always churned up, always mucky from their trampling there. They were farming people, had their main meal in the middle of the day, had rows. Her father vanished one night after supper, said he was going to count the cattle, brought a flashlamp, never came back. Others sympathized, but she and her mother were secretly relieved. Maybe he drowned himself in one of the many bog lakes, or changed his name and went to a city. At any rate he did not hang himself from a tree or do anything ridiculous like that.

She lay on her back as the instructor brought her across the pool, his hand under her spine. The sky above an innocent blightless blue with streamers where the jets had passed over. She let her head go right back. She thought, If I were to give myself to it totally, it would be a pleasure and an achievement, but she couldn't.

Argoroba hung from the trees like blackened banana skins. The men picked them in the early morning and packed them in sacks for winter fodder. In the barn where these sacks were stored there was a smell of decay. And an old olive press. In the linen room next door a pleasant smell of linen. The servants used too much bleach. Clothes lost their sharpness of colour after one wash. She used to sit in one or other of these rooms and read. She went to the library for a book. He was in one of the Regency chairs that was covered with ticking. As on a throne. One chair was real and one a copy but she could never tell them apart. 'I saw you yesterday, and you nearly went under,' he said. 'I still have several lessons to go,' she said, and went as she intended, but without the book that she had come to fetch.

His daughter by his third marriage had an eighteen-inch waist. On her first evening she wore a white trouser suit. She held the legs out and the small pleats when opened were like a concertina. At table she sat next to her father and gazed at him with appropriate awe. He told a story of a dangerous leopard hunt. They had lobster as a special treat. The lobster tails, curving from one place setting to the next, reached far more cordially than the conversation. She tried to remember something she had read that day. She found that by memorizing things she could amuse them at table.

'The gorilla resorts to eating, drinking or scratching to by-pass anxiety,' she said later. They all laughed.

'You don't say,' he said, with a sneer. It occurred to her that if she were to become too confident he would not want that either. Or else he had said it to reassure his daughter.

There were moments when she felt confident. She knew in her mind the movements she was required to make in order to pass through the water. She could not do them but she knew what she was supposed to do.

She worked her hands under the table, trying to make deeper and deeper forays into the atmosphere. No one caught her at it. The word plankton would not leave go of her. She saw dense masses of it, green and serpentine, enfeebling her fingers. She could almost taste it.

His last wife had stitched a backgammon board in green and red. Very beautiful it was. The fat woman played with him after dinner. They carried on the game from one evening to the next. They played very contentedly. The woman wore a different arrangement of rings at each sitting and he never failed to admire, and compliment her on them. To those not endowed with beauty he was particularly charming.

Her curling tongs fused the entire electricity system. People rushed out of their bedrooms to know what had happened. He did not show his anger but she felt it. Next morning they had to send a telegram to summon an electrician. In the telegram office two men sat, one folding the blue pieces of paper, one applying gum with a narrow brush and laying thin borders of white over the blue and pressing down with his hands. On the white strips the name and address had already been printed. The motor-cycle was indoors, to protect the tyres from the sun, or in case it might be stolen. The men took turns when a telegram had to be delivered. She saved one or other of them a journey because a telegram from a departed guest arrived while she was waiting. It simply said 'Thanks, Harry.' Guests invariably forgot something and in their thank-you letters mentioned what they had forgotten. She presumed that some of the hats stacked into one another and laid on the stone ledge were hats forgotten or thrown away. She had grown quite attached to a green one that had lost its ribbons.

The instructor asked to be brought to the souvenir shop. He bought a glass ornament and a collar for his dog. On the way back a man at the petrol station gave one of the children a bird. They put it in the chapel. Made a nest for it. The servant threw it nest and all into the wastepaper basket. That night at supper the talk was of nothing else. He remembered his fish story and he told it to the new people who had come, how one morning he had to abandon his harpoon because the lines got tangled, and next day, when he went back, he found that the shark had retreated into the cave and had two great lumps of rock in his mouth, where obviously he had bitten to free himself. That incident had a profound effect on him.

'Is the boat named after your mother?' she asked of his daughter. Her mother's name was Beth and the boat was called *Miss Beth*. 'He never said,' the daughter replied. She always disappeared after lunch. It must have been to accommodate them. Despite the heat they made a point of going to his room. And made a point of inventiveness. She tried a strong green stalk, to excite him, marvelling at it, comparing him and it. He watched. He could not endure such competition. With her head upside down and close to the tiled floor she saw all the oils and ointments on his bathroom ledge and tried reading their labels backwards. Do I like all this love-making? she asked herself. She had to admit that possibly she did not, that it went on too long, that it was involvement she sought, involvement and threat.

They swapped dreams. It was her idea. He was first.

Everyone was careful to humour him. He said in a dream a dog was lost and his grief was great. He seemed to want to say more but didn't, or couldn't. Repeated the same thing in fact. When it came to her turn she told a different dream from the one she had meant to tell. A short, uninvolved little dream.

In the night she heard a guest sob. In the morning the same guest wore a flame dressing-gown and praised the marmalade which she ate sparingly.

She asked for the number of lessons to be increased. She had three a day and she did not go on the boat with the others. Between lessons she would walk along the shore. The pine trunks were white as if a lathe had been put to them. The winds of winter the lathe. In winter they would move; to catch up with friends, business meetings, art exhibitions, to buy presents, to shop. He hated suitcases, he liked clothes to be waiting wherever he went, and they were. She saw a wardrobe with his winter clothes neatly stacked, she saw his frieze cloak with the black astrakhan collar and she experienced such a longing for that impossible season, that impossible city, and his bulk inside the cloak as they set out in the cold to go to a theatre. Walking along the shore she did the swimming movements in her head. It had got into all her thinking. Invaded her dreams. Atrocious dreams about her mother, father, and one where lion cubs surrounded her as she lay on a hammock. The cubs were waiting to pounce the second she moved. The hammock of course was unsteady. Each time she wakened from one of those dreams she felt certain that her cries were the repeated cries of infancy, and it was then she helped herself to the figs she had brought up.

He put a handkerchief, folded like a letter, before her plate at table. On opening she found some sprays of fresh mint, wide-leafed and cold. He had obviously put it in the refrigerator first. She smelt it and passed it round. Then on impulse she got up to kiss him and on her journey back nearly bumped into the servant with a tureen of soup, so excited was she.

Her instructor was her friend. 'We're winning, we're winning,' he said. He walked from dawn onwards, walked the hills and saw the earth with dew on it. He wore a handkerchief on his head that he knotted over the ears, but as he approached the house he removed this head-dress. She met him on one of these morning walks. As it got nearer the time she could neither sleep nor make love. 'We're winning, we're winning.' He always said it no matter where they met.

They set out to buy finger bowls. In the glass factory there were thin boys with very white skin who secured pieces of glass with pokers and thrust them into the stoves. The whole place smelt of wood. There was chopped wood in piles, in corners. Circular holes were cut along the top of the wall between the square grated windows. The roof was high and yet the place was a furnace. Five kittens with tails like rats lay bunched immobile in a heap. A boy, having washed himself in one of the available buckets of water, took the kittens one by one and dipped them in. She took it to be an act of kindness. Later he bore a hot blue bubble at the end of a poker and laid it before her. As the flame subsided it became mauve, and as it cooled more it was almost colourless. It had the shape of a sea serpent and an unnaturally long tail. Its colour and

Paradise

its finished appearance was an accident, but the gift was
clearly intentioned. There was nothing she could do
but smile. As they were leaving she saw him wait, near
the motor-car, and as she got in, she waved, wanly.
That night they had asparagus which is why they went
to the trouble to get finger bowls. These were blue
with small bubbles throughout, and though the
bubbles may have been a defect, they gave to the thick
glass an illusion of frost.

There was a new dog, a mongrel, in whom he took
no interest. He said the servants got new dogs simply
because he allotted money for that. But as they were
not willing to feed more than one animal, the previous
year's dog was either murdered or put out on the mountain. All these dogs were of the same breed, part wolf;
she wondered if when left on the mountain they re-
verted to being wolves. He said solemnly to the table
at large that he would never allow himself to become
attached to another dog. She said to him directly, 'Is it
possible to know beforehand?' He said, 'Yes.' She could
see that she had irritated him.

He came three times and afterwards coughed badly.
She sat with him and stroked his back, but when the
coughing took command he moved her away. He
leaned forward holding a pillow to his mouth. She saw
a film of his lungs, orange shapes with insets of dark that
boded ill. She wanted to do some simple domestic thing
like give him milk and honey but he sent her away.
Going back along the terrace she could hear the birds.
The birds were busy with their song. She met the
fat woman. 'You have been derouted,' the woman said,
'and so have I.' And they bowed mockingly.

Paradise

An archaeologist had been on a dig where a wooden temple was discovered. 'Tell me about your temple,' she said.

'I would say it's 400 B.C.,' he said, nothing more. Dry, dry.

A boy who called himself Jasper and wore mauve shirts received letters under the name of John. The letters were arranged on the hall table, each person's under a separate stone. Her mother wrote to say they were anxiously awaiting the good news. She said she hoped they would get engaged first but admitted that she was quite prepared to be told that the marriage had actually taken place. She knew how unpredictable he was. Her mother managed a poultry farm in England and was a compulsive eater.

Young people came to ask if Clay Sickle was staying at the house. They were in rags, but it looked as if they were rags worn on purpose and for effect. Their shoes were bits of motor-tyre held up with string. They all got out of the car though the question could have been asked by any one of them. He was on his way back from the pool and after two minute's conversation he invited them for supper. He throve on new people. That night they were the ones in the limelight – the three unkempt boys and the long-haired girl. The girl had very striking eyes which she fixed on one man and then another. She was determined to compromise one of them. The boys described their holiday, being broke, the trouble they had with the car which was owned by a hire purchase firm in London. After dinner an incident occurred. The girl followed one of the men into the bathroom. 'Want to see what you've got there,' she said and insisted upon watching while the man peed. She said they would do any kind of fucking he wanted.

She said he would be a slob not to try. It was too late
to send them away, because earlier on they'd been
invited to spend the night and beds were put up, down
in the linen room. The girl was the last to go over there.
She started a song 'All around his cock he wears a tri-
coloured rash-eo', and she went on yelling it as she
crossed the courtyard and went down the steps, bran-
dishing a bottle.

In the morning, she determined to swim by herself.
It was not that she mistrusted her instructor but the
time was getting closer, and she was desperate. As she
went to the pool one of the youths appeared in bor-
rowed white shorts, eating a banana. She greeted him
with faltering gaiety. He said it was fun to be out before
the others. He had a big head with closely cropped hair,
a short neck, and a very large nose.

'Beaches are where I most want to be, where it all
began,' he said. She thought he was referring to Crea-
tion and upon hearing such a thing he laughed, pro-
fanely. 'Let's suppose there's a bunch of kids and you're
all horsing around with a ball and all your sensory
dimensions are working ...'

'What?' she said.

'A hard on ...'

'Oh ...'

'Now the ball goes into the sea and I follow and she
follows me and takes the ball from my hand and a
dense rain of energy, call it love, from me to her and
vice versa, reciprocity in other words ...'

Sententious idiot. She thought, Why do people like
that have to be kept under his roof? Where is his judge-
ment, where? She walked back to the house, furious at
having to miss her chance to swim.

Dear Mother: It's not that kind of relationship. Being unmarried instals me as positively as being married and neither instals me with any certainty. It is a beautiful house but staying here is quite a strain. You could easily get filleted. Friends do it to friends. The food is good. Others cook it but I am responsible for each day's menu. Shopping takes hours. The shops have a special smell that is impossible to describe. They are all dark so that the foodstuffs won't perish. An old woman goes along the street in a cart selling fish. She has a very penetrating cry. It is like the commencement of a song. There are always six or seven little girls with her, they all have pierced ears, and wear fine gold sleepers. Flies swarm round the cart even when it is upright in the square. Living off scraps and fish scales, I expect. We do not buy from her, we go to the harbour and buy directly from the fishermen. The guests – all but one woman – eat small portions. You would hate it. All platinum people. They have a canny sense of self-preservation; they know how much to eat, how much to drink, how far to go; you would think they invented somebody like Shakespeare so proprietary are they about his talent. They are not fools – not by any means. There is a chessboard of ivory and it is so large it stands on the floor. Seats of the right height are stationed round it.

Far back – in my most distant childhood, Mother – I remember your nightly cough, it was a lament really and I hated it. At the time I had no idea that I hated it, which goes to show how unreliable feelings are. We do not know what we feel at the time and that is very perplexing. Forgive me for mentioning the cough, it is simply that I think it is high time we spoke our minds on all matters. But don't worry. You are centuries ahead of the people here. In a nut shell they brand you as idiot if you are harmless. There are jungle laws which you never taught me; you couldn't, you never knew them. Ah well!

I will bring you a present. Probably something suede. He says the needlework here is appalling and that things fall to pieces, but you can always have it re-made. We had some nice china jelly moulds when I was young. Whatever happened to them? Love.

Like the letter to the doctor it was not posted. She didn't tear it up or anything, it just lay in an envelope and she omitted to post it one day to the next. This new tendency disturbed her. This habit of postponing everything. It was as if something vital had first to be gone through. She blamed the swimming.

The day the pool was emptied she missed her three lessons. She could hear the men scrubbing and from time to time she walked down and stood over them as if her presence could hurry the proceedings and make the water flow in, in one miracle burst. He saw how she fretted, he said they should have had two pools built. He asked her to come with them on the boat. The books and the sun-oil were as she had last seen them. The cliffs as intriguing as ever. 'Hello cliff, can I fall off you?' She waved merrily. In a small harbour they saw another millionaire with his girl. They were alone, without even a crew. And for some reason it went straight to her heart. At dinner the men took bets as to who the girl was. They commented on her prettiness though they had hardly seen her. The water filling into the pool sounded like a stream from a faraway hill. He said it would be full by morning.

Other houses had beautiful objects but theirs was in the best taste. The thing she liked most was the dull brass chandelier, from Portugal. In the evenings when it was lit the cones of light tapered towards the rafters and she thought of wood smoke and the wings of birds endlessly fluttering. Votive. To please her he had a fire lit in a far-off room simply to have the smell of wood smoke in the air.

The watercress soup that was to be a speciality tasted like salt water. Nobody blamed her but afterwards she sat at table and wondered how it had gone wrong. She felt defeated. On request he brought another bottle of red wine but asked if she was sure she ought to have more. She thought, He does not understand the workings of my mind. But then, neither did she. She was drunk. She held the glass out. Watching the meniscus, letting it tilt from side to side, she wondered how drunk she would be when she stood up. 'Tell me,' she said, 'what interests you?' It was the first blunt question she had ever put to him.

'Why, everything,' he said.

'But deep down,' she said.

'Discovery,' he said, and walked away.

But not self-discovery, she thought, not that.

A neurologist got drunk and played jazz on the chapel organ. He said he could not resist it, there were so many things to press. The organ was stiff from not being used.

She retired early. Next day she was due to swim for them. She thought he would come to visit her. If he did they would lie in one another's arms and talk. She would knead his poor worn scrotum and ask questions about the world beneath the sea where he delved each day, ask about those depths and if there were flowers of some sort down there, and in the telling he would be bound to tell her about himself. She kept wishing for the organ player to fall asleep. She knew he would not come until each guest had retired because he was strangely reticent about his loving.

But the playing went on. If anything the player gathered strength and momentum. When at last he did fall asleep she opened the shutters. The terrace lights were all on. The night breathlessly still. Across the fields came the lap from the sea and then the sound of a sheep bell tentative and intercepted. Even a sheep recognized the dead of night. The light-house worked faithfully as a heart beat. The dog lay in the chair, asleep, but with his ears raised. On other chairs were sweaters and books and towels, the remains of the day's activities. She watched and she waited. He did not come. She lamented that she could not go to him on the night she needed him most.

For the first time she thought about cramp.

In the morning she took three headache pills and swallowed them with hot coffee. They disintegrated in her mouth. Afterwards she washed them down with soda water. There was no lesson because the actual swimming performance was to be soon after breakfast. She tried on one bathing suit, then another, then realizing how senseless this was she put the first one back on and stayed in her room until it was almost the time.

When she came down to the pool they were all there, ahead of her. They formed quite an audience: the twenty house guests and the six complaining children who had been obliged to quit the pool. Even the house-keeper stood on the stone seat under the tree, to get a view. Some smiled, some were a trifle embarrassed. The pregnant woman gave her a medal for good luck. It was attached to a pin. So they were friends. Her instructor stood near the front, the rope coiled round his wrist just in case. The children gave to the occasion its only levity. She went down the ladder backwards and looked at no face in particular. She crouched until the water covered her shoulders, then she gave a short leap and delivered herself to it. Almost at once she knew that she was going to do it. Her hands no longer loath to delve deep scooped the water away, and she kicked with a ferocity she had not known to be possible. She was aware of cheering but it did not matter about that. She swam, as she had promised, across the width of the pool in the shallow end. It was pathetically short, but it was what she had vouched to do. Afterwards one of the children said that her face was torture. The rubber flowers had long since come off her bathing cap, and she pulled it off as she stood up and held on to the ladder. They clapped. They said it called for a celebration. He said nothing but she could see that he was pleased. Her instructor was the happiest person there.

When planning the party they went to the study where they could sit and make lists. He said they would order gipsies and flowers and guests and caviare and swans of ice to put the caviare in. None of it would be her duty. They would get people to do it. In all, they wrote out twenty telegrams. He asked how she felt. She admitted that being able to swim bore little relation to not being able. They were two unreconcilable feelings. The true thrill she said was the moment when she knew she would master it but had not yet achieved it with her body. He said he looked forward to the day when she went in and out of the water like a knife. He did the movement deftly with his hand. He said next thing she would learn was riding. He would teach her himself or he would have her taught. She remembered the chestnut mare with head raised, nostrils searching the air, and she herself unable to stroke it, unable to stand next to it without exuding fear.

'Are you afraid of nothing?' she asked, too afraid to tell him specifically about the encounter with the mare which took place in his stable.

'Sure, sure.'

'You never reveal it.'

'At the time I'm too scared.'

'But afterwards, afterwards...' she said.

'You try to live it down,' he said and looked at her and hurriedly took her in his arms. She thought, Probably he is as near to me as he has been to any living person and that is not very near, not very near at all. She knew that if he chose her that they would not go in the deep end, the deep end that she dreaded and dreamed of. When it came to matters inside of himself he took no risks.

She was tired. Tired of the life she had elected to go into, and disappointed with the man she had put pillars round. The tiredness came from inside and like a deep breath going out slowly it tore at her gut. She was sick of her own predilection for rotten eggs. It seemed to her that she always held people to her ear, the way her mother held eggs, shaking them to guess at their rottenness, but unlike her mother she chose the very ones that she would have been wise to throw away. He seemed to sense her sadness but he said nothing, he held her and squeezed her from time to time in reassurance.

Her dress – his gift – was laid out on the bed, its wide white sleeves hanging down at either side. It was of open-work and it looked uncannily like a corpse. There was a shawl to go with it, and shoes and a bag. The servant was waiting. Beside the bath her book, an ash-tray, cigarettes, and a box of little soft matches that were hard to strike. She lit a cigarette and drew on it heartily. She regretted not having brought up a drink. She felt like a drink at that moment and in her mind she sampled the drink she might have had. The servant knelt down to put in the stopper. She asked that the bath should not be run just yet. Then she took the biggest towel and put it over her bathing suit, and went along the corridor, and down by the back stairs. She did not have to turn on the lights, she would have known her way, blindfolded, to that pool. All the toys were on the water, like farm animals just put to bed. She picked them out one by one and laid them at the side near the pile of empty chlorine bottles. She went down the ladder backwards.

She swam in the shallow end and confronted the thought that had urged to be thought for days. She thought, I shall do it, or I shall not do it, and the fact that she was in two minds about it seemed to confirm her view of the unimportance of the whole thing. Any-one, even the youngest child, could have persuaded her not, because her mind was without conviction. It just seemed easier, that was all, easier than the strain and the incomplete loving and the excursions that lay ahead.

'This is what I want, this is where I want to go,' she said, restraining that part of herself that might scream. Once she went deep, and she submitted to it, the water gathered all around in a great beautiful bountiful baptism. As she went down to the cold and thrilling region she thought, They will never know, they will never, ever know, for sure.

At some point she began to fight and thresh about,

and she cried though she could not know the extent of those cries.

She came to her senses on the ground at the side of the pool, all muffled up and retching. There was an agonizing pain in her chest as if the black frosts of winter had got in there. The servants were with her and two of the guests and him. The floodlights were on around the pool. She put her hands to her breast to make sure; yes she was naked under the blanket. They would have ripped her bathing suit off. He had obviously been the one to give respiration because he was breathing quickly and his sleeves were rolled up. She looked at him. He did not smile. There was the sound of music, loud, ridiculous and hearty. She remembered first the party, then, everything. The nice vagueness quit her and she looked at him with shame. She looked at all of them. What things had she shouted as they brought her back to life? What thoughts had they spoken in those crucial moments? How long did it take? Her immediate concern was they must not carry her to the house, she must not allow that last episode of indignity. But they did. As she was borne along by him and the gardener she could see the flowers and the oysters and jellied dishes and the small roast piglets all along the tables, a feast as in a dream, except that she was dreadfully clear-headed. Once alone in her room she vomited.

For two days she did not appear downstairs. He sent up a pile of books and when he visited her he always brought someone. He professed a great interest in the novels she had read and asked how the plots were. When she did come down the guests were polite and off hand and still specious, but along with that they were cautious now and deeply disapproving. Their manner told her that it had been a stupid and ghastly thing to do and had she succeeded she would have involved all of them in her stupid and ghastly mess. She wished she could go home, without any farewells. The children looked at her and from time to time laughed out loud. One boy told her that his brother had once tried to drown him in the bath. Apart from that and the inevitable letter to the gardener it was never mentioned. The gardener had been the one to hear her cry and raise the alarm. In their eyes he would be a hero.

People swam less. They made plans to leave. They had ready-made excuses – work, the change in the weather, aeroplane bookings. He told her that they would stay until all the guests had gone, and that then they would leave immediately. His secretary was travelling with them. He asked each day how she felt, but when they were alone he either read or played patience. He appeared to be calm except that his eyes blazed as with fever. They were young eyes. The blue seemed to sharpen in colour once the anger in him was resurrected. He was snappy with the servants. She knew that when they got back to London there would be separate cars waiting for them at the airport. It was only natural. The house, the warm flagstones, the shimmer of the water would accompany her and be a joy long after their love had become an echo.

More about Penguins

Penguinews, which appears every month, contains details of all the new books issued by Penguins as they are published. From time to time it is supplemented by *Penguins in Print*, which is a complete list of all books published by Penguins which are in print. (There are well over three thousand of these.)

A specimen copy of *Penguinews* will be sent to you free on request, and you can become a subscriber for the price of the postage – 30p for a year's issues (including the complete lists) if you live in the United Kingdom, or 60p if you live elsewhere. Just write to Dept EP, Penguin Books Ltd, Harmondsworth, Middlesex, enclosing a cheque or postal order, and your name will be added to the mailing list.

Some other books published by Penguins are described on the following pages.

Note: *Penguinews* and *Penguins in Print* are not available in the U.S.A. or Canada

August is a Wicked Month

Edna O'Brien

Ellen was alone, separated from her husband. Even her
son had to be shared.

Alone in London. And London was a place of loneliness
and frustration – a place that denied her a past, and
offered her no future.

So Ellen went south in search of sun and sex . . .

But is it ever quite as easy as that?

Not for sale in the U.S.A.

Casualties of Peace

Edna O'Brien

Willa had loved. Had been mangled by love. Wrung dry
enough to crack. Her desperation mirrored in the world
of glass she built to filter out the threat of feeling. With
Tom and Patsy, to secure a kind of peace. But outside
there was Auro. Inside, the need of Patsy to be free. And
between them all, the ultimate fragility of glass when the
tension finally snaps.

'. . . For laying, loving, sheer high spirits – and for a
sweet vulnerability – a fear of time the enemy of
beautiful women – there hasn't been a book like this one
since the last Edna O'Brien' – *Punch*

Not for sale in the U.S.A.

The Country Girls

Edna O'Brien's famous first novel introduces us to Kate and Baba, the delightful heroines of an engaging trilogy.

'*The Country Girls*, with its unphoney charm and unlaborious originality, wins my personal first-novel prize of the year' – Kingsley Amis in the *Observer*.

'Miss O'Brien has a crisp eye and unaffected good-humour . . . a shrewd eye for oddity and the telling detail. Her descriptions of the countryside, the decaying mortgaged house, the convent, are firm and lively: so are her portraits: hard-drinking father, nuns, German landlady, Dublin businessmen on the batter – conventional types but freshly seen . . . A buoyantly youthful novel, with all the freshness in the world and undertones of something more lasting' – Storm Jameson in the *Sunday Times*.

'Excellent and highly unusual blend of bawdiness and innocence' – *Evening Standard*.

Long after you've finished reading *The Country Girls*, its mixture of knowledgeable purity, wide-eyed devilment, and sheer unadulterated *joie de vivre* will linger on in your mind.

Not for sale in the U.S.A. or Canada

Girl with Green Eyes

Edna O'Brien

The continued adventures of Caithleen Brady and her
friends, now based on Dublin's fair city, again prised the
critics out of their seats with a display of comical and
poignant effects. Let *The Times Literary Supplement*
speak for them all: 'Few women writers have written
so unselfconsciously, and at the same time with such
enchanting ribaldry, about a girl in love.'

Not for sale in the U.S.A. or Canada

Girls in their Married Bliss

Edna O'Brien

Tearful Kate — bored with her grey husband in their
grey stone house in the country — is driven to indiscretions
she can hardly handle without Baba's help.
And Baba already has her own hands full – keeping one
step ahead of the unpredictable passions of her rich and
vulgar builder . . .

Not for sale in the U.S.A or Canada

The Fetish and Other Stories

Alberto Moravia

There's a man who goes through the tortured charade of reconstructing a dead love affair . . . a husband with the compulsion to spend an innocent night in the bed of his wife from whom he is separated . . . the wife who finds that the dead body on the beach means far more to her than she dreamt . . . In brilliant lightning-flashes of imagination Alberto Moravia reveals a world of oddities – oddities made up of bits of us all.

and also in Penguins by Alberto Moravia:

Bitter Honeymoon and Other Stories
The Conformist   Conjugal Love
The Empty Canvas   The Fancy Dress Party
Two Adolescents   Two Women
The Wayward Life and Other Stories
The Woman of Rome   A Ghost at Noon

Not for sale in U.S.A.